MONSTERS

MONSTERS

A
PHOENIX QUILL
ANTHOLOGY

Edited by Ashley Cyr

MONSTERS: AN ANTHOLOGY

Copyright © 2016 Ashley Cyr

Cover by: John Ryers

ISBN-13: 978-0-9952890-1-7
ISBN-10: 0-9952890-1-8

Bushmead Publishing
www.bushmead.com

Printed in U.S.A.

To all of those
who've had to deal with monsters
in one form, or another.

TABLE OF CONTENTS

An Introduction

Monsters come in all shapes and sizes. They are what we are afraid of, what haunts us. No matter where they come from, they hold a fascination for humanity. Our eyes are always attracted to the dark spot, watching for something that is going to jump out and get us. Survival instincts, now so seldom needed compared to our past, keep us vigilant. Come with us as we march into the darkness, serving as a humble guide through a small zoo of monsters. Perhaps you'll recognize some, and perhaps we still have some secrets in store for you.

- Bushmead, October 2016

CLEARANCE
BY CHRIS MUSGRAVE

The crack of a pistol shot started it all. So loud it caused my ears to ring. So close that the pulse of hot expanding air scorched my bare cheek. First one shot and then another.

We surged forward, firing, killing, dying. Our shots were chosen with care, with a deadly strategy in mind. Bullets struck not only the opposing ranks but also those standing to the left and right, anyone closer to the prize than the shooters themselves.

Blood ran from open wounds, spread and blossomed across the fabric of loose clothing. Startled bodies gave out only to be trampled by those behind.

When guns ran dry, they were discarded. Their owners descended upon each other with knives and claws. Steel and bone pierced flesh. Wounds like lipless mouths opened, vomiting black blood and bile onto the floor. I couldn't make myself look away.

I went down when my foot found the spreading viscera, nearly lost my pistol. The hand I used to steady myself came away wet, sticky.

A thick miasma hung in the air. An eddying, fetid smog of copper gore and sharp excrement. It reached down my throat to twist at my stomach, forcing its acidic contents up into my mouth.

The few of us that remained hid behind rows of metal

shelves. I was alone, lying low beneath the bodies. Their cooling flesh caressed my bare calves. Lifeless appendages draped over me in limp, protective embraces.

The prize hung before me, no more than ten hurried steps away, but all of that open ground. I'd be cut down if I moved and so I remained still, watched for an opening.

Bestial screams echoed through the space. Each cut short by the thrust of a weapon or a wet thump of something solid striking flesh. I counted seven more dead by the sounds alone.

Movement near me. The scrape of heels on stone preceded the dull thud of disturbed bodies. So close that I daren't look around.

They were looking for me, for survivors. Two sets of footsteps approached, one from each side. Any closer and they would have spotted me.

My fingers tightened involuntarily around the grip of my handgun. My free hand inched towards the handle of a dropped knife soaking in a glistening pool of dark blood.

They were right on top of me. I held my breath for fear they'd hear. The toes of a shoe pressed into the flesh over my ribs. Heart beating fast, I readied the knife to strike.

I don't know what saved me. Whether it was a noise that drew their attention or the confidence that they were the only ones remaining. Whatever the cause, they retreated, circling around to either side of my position. The set on my right paused momentarily, just long enough to retrieve a revolver from the floor.

When they came into view, I was surprised at how young they looked. A redhead and a brunette. Neither could have been out of their teens. Dark miniskirts, gore-slicked blouses, and how did they wade through this in six-inch stilettos?

They met in the middle of the aisle and regarded each other with wide, excited eyes, sharing a congratulatory hug. A friendship reinforced through victory. Hand in hand, they set out to claim their prize.

The dress was one of a kind. A masterpiece of colour, silk still wrinkled by its creator's rough fingers. It had travelled all the way from Milan — further than the two girls had likely travelled in their combined years. This season's latest outfit at a price you'd kill for.

In silent reverence, they each reached out a hand to touch it, their eyes wet with joyful tears. They eased the dress down from the rack, careful to keep the hem high and away from the bloodied floor.

"It's so beautiful," one whispered. She was so fixated on the garment that she missed the gun in her friend's left hand, creeping slowly up toward her temple.

The shot caused her head to snap sideways. Only the quick reaction of the redhead prevented the dress from following her friend into the gore. That was my chance.

I was on my feet before she completed her turn, but she was faster at bringing a weapon to bear. I winced, tensing to receive the fiery slug.

Two hollow clicks. The hammer impacting spent rounds. Better luck next year, I thought, and my own gun bucked once in my hand.

Bitter cordite filled my nostrils at almost the same time a perfectly circular, red hole appeared on the redhead's brow. The thinnest bead of pale blood traced a line from it, hugging the side of her nose like a sinister tear.

Did I tell you how much I'd loved that dress? Ever since I'd first laid eyes on it, I knew I had to have it. And now, it was mine. I had so many plans for it, so many chances to show it off.

What a bargain you can get in the sales.

MOHUN

BY JOHN RYERS

I can't remember a time I wasn't hunting monsters.

My earliest memory is of my father throwing me into a pit of Valusion Rippers with a sixty-year-old pulse rifle I could barely lift. My mother watched from the edge, yelling to hurry my ass up and shoot the buggers before dinner got cold. So I did.

Monster hunting was in my family's blood. We were born into it and died from it. My father took his final breath between the jaws of a Tarlan Rusk. It ripped him clean in half and I swear he winked at me while it happened. Mother didn't go so nonchalantly. I learned at least twice as many curse words than I thought existed the day she died. Both fine parents, both fine deaths, but far too young an age to die. I'd always hoped to do a little more with my life before cashing out.

So when the bounty came up for a Zanark in the Theda Quadrant, I thought it'd be a good way to go. Monster Hunters, or Mohuns as they called us in the inner circles, didn't mess with Zanarks unless they had a death wish. Despite their ridiculous name, there was nothing funny about going up against one. I'd seen men empty entire clips of phazon plasma or launch cluster rockets directly into a Zanark's head, only to watch it grin before dismembering each and every one of them.

That was in the early days when I ran. Everyone runs at first.

How could you not with a dozen arms and razor-sharp claws sprinting after you? But Mohuns who ran didn't last long in the game. They either died with their backs to a beast, or became known as cowards, which was probably worse since bounties weren't given out to those with such deplorable reputations.

My one-man ship I lovingly named *The Piss*, rumbled toward the space station where Admiral Primus resided. He had more wealth than anyone this side of the Belt Horizon, and had no problem putting nearly half his fortune up when a Zanark took up residence in the bowels of his mining colony. He was a proud man, but not stupid enough to tackle the Zanark himself, and that's where I came in. He wasn't keen on dying and I wasn't keen on empty pockets, so there was mutual benefit in me dealing with his problem.

The Piss pulled into a dock and after a rumble, a hiss, and a couple locks popping, I was inside the station. Two fully armoured guards with pulse rifles in their hands and pickles up their asses escorted me to the admiral's chambers. They'd last about seventeen seconds against a Zanark.

The doors slid apart revealing the admiral sitting behind a desk much too large for one person. Plants adorned the desktop on either side of him and he spritzed one with water as I entered. Plants were fancy, luxury items these days. Anyone who owned one was loaded, and often people killed for the things. I never had much luck with plants. I tried to grow one once from a sprout I'd traded a ship for. Thought I'd have it made, selling its seeds for piles of checkings. Bloody thing died in three days.

"It's a rose," the admiral said, as we both looked at the thorny plant beside him. "Cost me two ships and a year of rations for that one. Beautiful, isn't it?"

"It's lovely," I said. "Now about the bounty."

"Yes, yes," he said, still staring at the plant. "Your clearance checks out and no one else has claimed it yet. But I suppose you know that, otherwise we wouldn't be having this conversation..."

His words hung as he stared at me and it suddenly occurred to me that he didn't know my name. I forgot sometimes how unknown I am to the rich. In the streets, everyone knew my name. But here, in the shiny and the clean, I was nothing. And that was perfect.

"Sams," I said. "Jazen Sams. My friends call me Sammy."

"Is that so?"

"No, not really. I don't have any friends."

He cracked half a smile as if laughing cost him money.

"The Zanark's in the lowest mine of Pit Three. They tell me she's the biggest they've ever seen. Smart. Cunning. Someone even swore they heard her speak. She's building a hive or something down there, I don't know. The scientific terms and explanations bore me. I just want it dead."

"A hive is probable if she's down that deep. But that'd also mean she's a queen. Queens are extra."

"Half a million checkings not enough for you, Sams?"

"Not really," I said.

It wasn't a clean half mil. I explained there was ammo to buy and weapons to use it with. Queens were particularly robust creatures that'd need a delicate mixture of tranquilizers, concussion blasts and incendiary devices to take down. Then there was fuel to get down to the surface. The anchors on *The Piss* would need realignment and fresh hydraulic fluid in case there was a wave storm while I was in the pit. Then all the rappelling gear. By the time all that was accounted for, hell I'd have used up half the bounty.

I could see the admiral's eyes glaze over. He really did hate extraneous details.

"An extra two-hundred thousand checkings for the queen."

The admiral nearly choked. "Ridiculous," he said and nodded to the guards who hadn't left the doorway.

"Suit yourself," I said. "But I'm charging double when you call me back in a month because your mining operation's shut down and every pit you own is overrun by Zanark spawn. Toodle-loo."

I had one foot out the door when he called me back in. I sat down and put my feet up on his desk, my hands behind my head.

"So we have a deal?"

"Take out the queen and you'll get what you've asked for," the admiral said with a scowl. "I'll give you half now and half when you return with her heart."

"You sure you want her heart? You know how bad those things smell, right?"

He stared at me blankly until it became awkward and I decided to leave.

"Wait," he said.

"Something else, Admiral?"

"You want an extra two-hundred thousand checkings, fine. I want something as well."

He waved over to a side door and it opened. A scrawny, little teenager walked through with a puffed out chest and hair slicked back against his head. His pointy little chin matched his pointy little eyebrows and he looked at me like I was a dog who'd just shit all over the floor.

"Father," he said to the admiral.

"Sams, this is my son, Nedrin. He'll be accompanying you down to Pit Three."

"Yeah, no. This works out a lot better if I do it alone."

"You altered our deal, Sams. I'm returning the favour. Nedrin has aspirations of becoming a Mohun himself. His mother disagrees but I side with Nedrin. What better way to get his name out there than to slay a Zanark queen for his father?"

"It won't end well for the kid," I said.

Nedrin didn't like that. Nedrin didn't like that at all. He glared and leaned on the desk, doing his best to look tough and menacing. "I'm first in my Mohun simulation class and I've passed every beast and monster encounter they've thrown at me."

"Simulation class?"

"They won't let us face the real things, but we've been assured the simulations are 99% real-world accurate."

"Ah, that's good," I said. "Then there's a 99% chance you're going to die."

"If you don't take Nedrin along, there's a 99% chance you'll leave with nothing," the admiral added.

"Fine," I said. "You want to be a Mohun? So be it."

This complicated things, but it could be handled easily enough. "Let's go," I said.

He followed me out as the admiral spritzed another plant.

Nedrin tapped his fingers on the ship's console as I poured a cup of coffee. "Are you quite finished, Mohun?"

I hadn't even taken a sip yet.

To hell with him and his father and his plants. If I was being forced to take a civilian along on a hunt, (a Zanark hunt no less) I wasn't doing it without a cup of high-grade, synthetic coffee. The galaxy wept when the last of the real coffee beans were gone. At least I'd like to think it did. I could talk about a good cup of java all day, but then that meant talking to Nedrin.

"Don't make me test the weapons on you, boy."

The brat huffed and folded his arms as he sat in my chair, the only seat in *The Piss*.

"Get out," I said.

He didn't move.

"If you think I'm flying this ship down to Pit Three from the cargo hold, you're more delusional than I thought."

He sighed and got up as slowly as a person possibly could, then glanced around. "Where am I supposed to sit?"

"On the wing if I had it my way," I said, then nodded to the small cargo bay.

I took pleasure strapping him against the crate wall. Leather buckles across his chest, waist and legs made him look like a psychopath ready for transport to the local prison. His wide eyes, full of disbelief that'd I'd force him to travel this way, only strengthened that look. But I wasn't going to have Nedrin bouncing all around *The Piss* during the descent. Blood was far too hard to clean off the controls and he'd have plenty of opportunity to bleed in Pit Three.

Thankfully for my own sanity, Nedrin's simulation training made him somewhat useful after the landing. He could perform duties that any third-rate rookie could do: loading ammo, anchoring *The Piss* to the rusted steel plates that covered most of Pit Three's surface. Hell, he even got dressed in the exo-suit required for the descent, all by himself. He was still going to die, but he'd die looking like a Mohun, which I could only assume was what he wanted out of this.

He wore a smug grin as the suit sparked to life with its telltale high-pitched energy charge. I couldn't fault him for that. An exo-suit coming to life was a pleasure. All the fancy, blinking lights flashing around like a goddamned beacon, calling any monsters to you like a fisherman's lure in an overstocked lake. There was nothing stealthy about an exo-suit, but that was the point. A Mohun wanted the beasts to come to them because it made things easier, and the easier a bounty was to claim, the richer you got. The admiral's son may be looking for glory, but I was looking for checkings. Many, many, oh-so-many checkings.

The Piss sealed itself with a pulse shield, and defensive guns popped out of several hatches to keep the area clear while we were off Zanark killing. There'd been a few hunts I'd returned from with heavy wounds and very little blood, but so long as you hit the big red button on the outside, *The Piss* did a damn fine job of getting you off-planet and away to the nearest medical station all by itself. Auto-pilot was a beautiful thing sometimes. I reminded Nedrin of this before we headed into Pit Three and he gave a half-assessed salute. "Sir, yes sir," he said through his helmet with a modulated voice.

I suited up as well and we began our descent with rapelling gear, using mini-thrusters on our boots when we had nowhere to anchor. In a pinch, we could escape the mining pit by turning the boots on full-blast and rocketing to the surface like superheroes. Fortunately (if there was anything fortunate about hunting a Zanark) the fact that this was a queen meant every other monster with any sense of self-preservation stayed out of her territory. This made the trip down clear, quick, and easy, with only Nedrin's complaining ruining an otherwise perfect-ten descent.

The lights embedded in the rocks by the miners still functioned, burning away some of the pitch-black surroundings so we could actually see.

"I hope there's Zanark spawn down here," he said as we both touched down in the deepest cavern.

"Hoping for a particularly painful death then?" I asked.

He gave that rookie look of confusion.

"Thought they would've taught you that in simulation school," I said, explaining to the lad that Zanark spawn were excellent at killing but not at all efficient like their mother. Picture a baby eating. They'd chomp down on you wildly, ripping limbs and entrails and other pieces of your body off as they clumsily shoved you in their mouths. The queens were far, far more efficient. They'd spike you with their tails and send a neurotoxin into your spine that'd incapacitate you in a few seconds. They'd drag you off, consume you whole, and you'd live in their digestive track for as long as you could hold your breath or until the acid melted your flesh from bone. You'd die quickly, but not quick enough.

Nedrin rolled his eyes behind the orange, tempered phazon glass of his visor. "Takes a lot more than a few slugs to scare me off, old-timer."

"I could shoot you now," I said. "No one would know."

I left the conversation at that and headed into the darkness, whistling the most inappropriate, upbeat tune I could remember. Nedrin grumbled a bit, but didn't say another word until we saw the eggs.

I hadn't seen this much potential death in one place since I stumbled upon a trezzen flock three years prior. Took every last plasma bolt I had to put the bastards down, but now, here in this cavern, well this was something else. Three dozen rows of eggs lined an open expanse of mined rock. The eggs were closed, thankfully, but they'd swollen to twice their resting size, meaning any day now the mine would fill with hundreds of starving Zanark larva. A single larva could devour a full-grown man in less than a minute. Not the best way to die. My father, if he were still alive, would shake his head at the thought of his son finding death in the intestinal tract of a worm. Mother would have a few choice words about it too.

"That's what I'm talking about," Nedrin said and gave a long whistle like he'd done this before. He held his rifle with a combat-ready grip, aiming at the nearest egg.

I grabbed his gun and lowered it before he killed us both. "We do this right," I said. "Set the incendiary charges along each row. I trust you ran a simulation for dealing with a Zanark hive?"

"Just once. But I aced it, naturally."

"Alright then, Ace. Get to it."

He steeled himself as any greener would in the presence of a seasoned Mohun and began setting the charges. One by one he placed them along the rows of eggs, being careful not to touch them. The egg's membrane was sensitive to physical touch and prone to burst at even the slightest bump, but Nedrin did well and half an hour later the bombs were ready for detonation.

"Do we really want to anger the queen," Nedrin asked, like I hadn't done this a hundred times before.

"We certainly do," I said and armed the devices. "A Zanark queen on the hunt is probably one of the most formidable forces in the galaxy, kid. We need to throw her off her game. You know, piss her off some. She'll expose her weaknesses that way and we'll see her coming a mile out."

"A mile out? Where's the fun in that?" Nedrin asked.

"Figure of speech, kid. Now shut up and set your suit to heat-deflection, unless of course you want to join the eggs in the

BBQ."

Nedrin nodded and poked a few buttons on his arm. The suit lit up with infrared deflection pads and glowed orange. I did the same and we took up position behind a large rock. This would help block most of the heat and allow a decent vantage point of the cavern the queen was no doubt hiding in.

"Care to do the honours?" I asked, holding out the trigger.

Nedrin scooped it up and looked at it in his hand for a moment. You could see the wheels turning in his head. The look in his eyes and the way he focused said it all: pushing that button would make him a Mohun, at least, in *his* eyes it would. That was the problem with spoiled little rich kids who had admirals for daddies: a click of a button was all it took for glory. Forget the years of training, the hundreds of close calls and the psychological toll it took knowing you were probably going to die on every hunt. Bloody kids these days.

Nedrin clicked the button. The air ignited and blinding fire and light consumed our surroundings. Torrents of flame roared and swirled around us and the eggs popped with squeals from the larva inside. And then it stopped. As quickly as the fire came it was gone, leaving an expanse of charred husks where eggs once were and ash flakes falling from above like snow. Peaceful, if not for the ear-piercing shriek of the queen.

"Switch suits to concussion deflection and your rifle to maximum output. Override the safety warning and tuck that sucker back into your shoulder. Don't fire until you see her underbelly."

"I know how to fight," Nedrin said, focusing on the queen's lair.

She should've come charging out of the cavern by now but things were different this time. Nedrin complicated things. Now there were two of us the Zanark had to deal with.

Queens were smart and this one was no exception. She waited in the shadows. You could see her there in the darkness, watching. Her carapace was thick as steel and glowed with luminescent patches of red and orange to match her dozen eyes. They scanned the expanse and stopped at the rock we hid behind.

Then she spoke.

"I can smell your fear, little one," she said. Her voice was only a whisper, yet it echoed in the air.

"Holy shit, they really *can* talk," Nedrin said.

The queen laughed.

"You've brought a gift, Mohun?" she asked. "Young, with blood full of fire. I thank you."

"Not by choice," I called out. "Followed me down against his better judgement. What say you let the kid go and deal with me?"

"I'm not going anywhere," Nedrin said. "This is what I've trained for."

"Look, kid, I appreciate your bravado, God knows I was the same at your age. But there's a lot of money riding on this hunt and if I return to your father with your digested corpse, I'll be leaving the Theda Quadrant with nothing, or worse."

"My father is an honourable man. He'll pay what's been agreed upon. We'll fight the Zanark queen together, Mohun. And together we'll win."

Touching sentiment if not a bit cliché, but the kid couldn't stick around if the plan was going to work. It wasn't the first time someone had tagged along on a Zanark hunt and it wouldn't be the last, at least, not for me. Most of the others would've run off by now, but the brat needed a little more convincing.

"Alright, here's the plan," I said and his face lit up with a smile. "If she gets you with her stinger, you're done. You'll lose feeling in your body and slump to the ground like a rag doll, but don't worry, you'll still be able to scream as she drags you back into her lair."

"So we neutralize the stinger," Nedrin said.

"We don't. I do," I corrected. "I told you queens were smart.

She'll focus on me because I'm the bigger threat. I've danced around a Zanark stinger once or twice before so while I'm doing that, you get one good shot between her hearts. She has two, you'll need to destroy them both to put her down."

"Won't be a problem, Mohun," Nedrin said. "Anything else?"

I shook my head. "This concludes our lesson of the day. Good luck and don't bloody-well die."

He nodded and charged his rifle, taking up position on the edge of the rock. He poked his head around the side and the queen noticed immediately. Time to play.

"Oy! You miserable bitch," I yelled, bounding around the rock and charging right for her. "Come and get me."

I fired a few warning shots into her side as I replayed the words in my head. Come and get me? What the hell was that, some sort of tribute to late-twentieth-century action movies? I'd come up with far better taunts in previous hunts. Nedrin must've been throwing me off my game.

The warning shots didn't seem to faze her much and she was still after the kid. "No," I called out. "Over here!"

A precision shot in between her eyes finally got her attention. She emerged from the shadows like a spider stalking flies in a web. Controlled. Patient. Her stinger unrolled off her back, the venom spike as long as my arm but thin like a rapier. A single glob of neurotoxin coated the tip.

"You won't survive," she hissed.

"It'd be an honour to die by you," I said, "but I'm not in the dying mood today."

She laughed and spiked the ground before my feet. She didn't miss; she'd done that on purpose. Toying with me and letting me know the odds were decidedly not in my favour. Another jab came a little too close for comfort so I dove aside, rolling and popping up with a charged plasma rifle. I put a single shot into her venom sac and it exploded, raining poison over my suit. A decent hit, but her stinger still held a dose of neurotoxin. Like Mohuns who'd accidentally killed themselves cleaning their plasma rifles because they still held a single charge in the chamber, the Zanark's stinger was no different and could still put a man down, venom sac or not.

Nedrin poked his head up from the rock and nodded toward the queen's underbelly.

It was a bad angle and his shot would deflect, leaving him wide open for a counterattack from the queen. You couldn't ask for a better setup, so I approved his silent question with a nod and he squeezed the trigger.

As predicted, the blast struck between the queen's hearts with impeccable aim but her carapace bounced the bolt away, leaving little more than a scorch mark. The Zanark turned toward Nedrin who, for the first time showed signs of panic. He fumbled to load another charge as the queen advanced on him with slow, calculated steps. He'd never get another shot in time.

I ran full out toward Nedrin as the queen stopped in front of him and rose up on her back two legs, reaching a height of nearly thirty feet. Her underbelly was exposed and open to a perfect shot between her hearts but Nedrin froze, his rifle still pointed at the ground and his terrified eyes locked on the stinger poised to strike.

She snapped it at Nedrin, but I managed to jump between him and the queen's attack. The barb caught me in the back of my thigh, piercing my exo-suit like a needle through butter. The venom coursed through me quick and the pain left as I crashed to the ground by Nedrin's feet. He looked at me with wide eyes that quivered with tears around the edges.

"Run, you idiot," I screamed.

The queen pulled me away from Nedrin, my body scraping over the ground and bouncing off the burnt out Zanark eggs. "Run," I yelled again but he only backed away slowly, like he'd forgotten how to use his legs, his eyes never leaving mine as the queen dragged me further and further away. It wasn't until the Zanark stopped and screeched right at the kid that he finally snapped out of it and ran.

He dropped the rifle, activated his boot thrusters and fled

from the cavern. He'd know how to get himself out of Pit Three and back to his father's station. So long as he didn't stop, he'd make it.

The queen finally stopped dragging me across the ground and let go, flipping me over on my back. She loomed over me, her head lowering until her mandibles were inches from my face.

"Are you hurt, Mohun?" she asked.

"Well I'm not sure," I said. "Your goddamned venom's done a number on my nerves this time. You've gotta work on your aim, sweetheart. Three inches higher and that spike of yours would've went straight up my ass."

"It was dark," she said.

"No excuses. Nice touch with the eggs by the way. Very creepy."

"I thought you'd like that, Mohun."

She picked me up and set my rag doll body against a large rock until the venom waned. She was good that way. Very motherly.

I'd met her as an egg during a hunt about a decade back. My original plan was to sell the egg on the black market for a thousand checkings, which was big money for a rookie back then. Zanark eggs contained a plethora of valuable fluids that could be extracted and turned into profitable narcotics. Problem was, the bloody egg hatched before I could close the deal.

The unsavoury folks I was dealing with thought I was trying to double-cross them and thus, in typical bad guy fashion, tried to kill me. The Zanark larva that'd just hatched intervened and ate them. I thought it might chew on me as well, but it seemed to take a liking to me. Completely uncharacteristic of a Zanark, it acted more like a lost puppy than a murderous bug and followed me all they way back to my ship.

I tried to lose her a few times over the following months,

dropping her off on various asteroids and scooting away in *The Piss*. She'd always find me. Always come back. But the last time I dropped her off somewhere, it was inhabited by civilians. I hadn't known this until receiving their distress call, and since it was sort of my bad, I'd decided to remove the Zanark and drop her off somewhere a little more desolate.

After I'd chased her away from the colony, their leader approached me with praise and a crate full of checkings for "saving his people." I was celebrated for three days by idiots who had no idea the Zanark was waiting patiently for me just outside the colony. It didn't take long to see the value in this.

"The little one took your ship," she said.

"Yeah. Figured that'd happen what with you trying to eat him and all."

"I'm hungry," she said.

"You can snack after I close the bounty. I'm gonna need you to fly me back to the station," I said, finally able to stand on my own. "I'm also going to need one of your hearts."

"It just grew back," she said.

"Yeah, that's kind of the point, love. Don't want you actually dying on me."

She cooed, lifting her carapace that shielded one of her hearts and sliced between the plates, screeching as she pulled the heart out, poor thing. It beat three times before going still and stunk like a thousand rotting fish as she handed it over.

"Seven-hundred-thousand checkings," I said. "Biggest haul yet. Can you believe it?"

"I am pleased for you, Mohun. You're sure he'll pay?" she asked, sealing up her incision with mucus.

"We made a deal, and now that I've saved his son's life, he couldn't possibly back out of it. Not unless he wants a certain Zanark queen to obliterate his station, right?"

I shot her a wink and she chirped.

"Where to next, Mohun?" she asked.

"I'm thinking we take a break from Theda Quadrant for a while. Gamma hasn't had any Zanark action in a couple years.

Might be time for a sighting, yeah?"

"I'll make my presence known," she said.

I smiled and climbed onto her back, and we left for the admiral's station.

I couldn't remember a time in my life I hadn't hunted monsters, but I wasn't going out like mom and dad. They loved the hunt. They loved the kills, and they loved getting killed by those that they obsessed over.

Me? I was a Mohun and had no interest in dying to a monster. Checkings were far better than glory these days and I was good at getting rich by exploiting other people's ignorance and fear. I'd done it before, and I'd happily do it again.

TAKING DOWN GOLIATH
BY DAVID WILEY

Canto I

She rides across the grassy plains, weary
from tough trials conquered the day before.
Her cheeks are pale and worn, green eyes bleary
and dull. Her fiery hair is matted with gore
proof of her fight with fierce monster, the war
betwixt two souls, their fates locked in stalemate.
Silver armor, once bright and strong, is scored
with scars from grip so tightly bound. The weight
from dark encounters fierce entwined within her fate.

That duel has forced her thoughts to turn inward,
toward newfound weakness, to face exposed
monster within. Her mind deemed this absurd,
these truths revealed – her Sin, hubris, imposed
and aimed toward her foes. Her heart opposed
this new revelation but found that naught
suppressed the thought. Inner turmoil now posed
a threat, immune to blade. Her mind was wrought,
Batt'ling this foe untouched by might – could it be fought?

Her state of soul is matched by looks. Her shield,
bearing a large amber cross, is battered
its shape deformed, layers of paint have peeled
from steel surface. She wears tunic, tattered
and frayed, once vibrant like fresh grass, splattered
with blood as black as moonless night. Grimy
layers of dust settled on skin, scattered
patches of soot fighting hard to stymie,
to mask features beneath that mark strength and beauty.

Razed fields of wheat smolder upon all sides,
dark smoke spiraling, caught within the air
from charred remains. This cloud of haze provides
perfect cover to cross the fields, a rare
chance for riding concealed. Her mind aware
yet blind, her eyes seeing damaged terrain
without recognizing meaning. Despair
lances throughout her thoughts, usurping reign
over her soul while horse gallops across the plain.

Two scouts appear amidst the smoke, blocking
the path. They cry out, "Halt," and draw their blades,
seeking answers to why she comes stalking
into the heart of fierce war, this crusade
between the King and wild monster brigade.
"This war against monster army," said she,
"is why I come. My skills may bring some aid.
Gladly will I defend my own country,
facing peril to serve royal King for a fee."

The two men shared a glance so brief, a look
of swift debate, before turning to her
with frowns on their faces. "You are a crook
turning our plight into profit. A cur
comes forth each day to taunt our troops, to stir
into action one brave man to combat

single to find the side that wins. Now spur
your horse and turn back now. This feud, this spat
our deaths could bring about. The wise would flee,
not chat."

Their plea this brave woman ignores. She leads
Her steed along the road. After riding
Down the winding trail she spies the deeds
of troops huddled around their tents, biding
their time. Dismounting horse, she goes striding
among soldiers. Their long faces express
absence of hope, they are here hiding
in fear. She finds new strength in their duress,
coming alive to be hero amidst distress.

Gathered within this group of men, the King
is found beside an oak table. Gray eyes
are fixed firmly upon a map, seeking
strategy wise to save all from demise.
His robes are torn, coated with ash, his guise
one of deepest lament. He bites cracked lips,
uttering words of prayer to seek advice
to guide his men safely from their hardship
or bold hero to take control with sponsorship.

He starts upon seeing her come and hope
flickers across his face. Her name he asks,
looking above. She says, "Why do you mope
as though this war is lost? Cast off this mask
worn of hopeless despair, rise to the task,
my lord, and lead your men! Be courageous
and bold!" He sighs and says, "I drown in flask
I shall until some man arrives, gracious
enough to fight my foe. None here are audacious.

"For days I stood, bereft of food and sleep,

poring over these maps, lifting prayers
pleading for one hero. Each night I weep
for lives now lost and wait for bold slayer
of beasts to come at last," he says. Aware
the king believes she will accept the fight
and thus relieve his men from plight, a snare
within her soul has shut. The weight of right
will bind her here. No foe will make her flee tonight.

Canto II

Vibrant thrumming of drums echoes across
the plains as there gather armies. No stream
nor tree between the two, and one could toss
a stone and hit the side across. The theme
was clear with both the camps, the men could dream
no way to win the war; monsters all thought
the end was here. They shout and cheer, they teem
and boast with pride; they taunt and jeer with naught
a care about the way this day of war is fought.

A shrill horn sounds, silence comes in its wake.
Goblins and orcs then part in waves to clear
The way for champ chosen to come and make
today's challenge. The fierce feelings of fear
consume the men before their foe draws near.
Their hearts flutter, their minds tainted, defiled
by days under the threat of death out here.
Suspense hovers over the scene, piled
upon them all until emotions are riled.

A dark figure towers over the lines
formed of cowering men, covering ground
swiftly with each great stride. Armor entwines
his large body. His balding head is crowned
with steel plates, encircling his round

face. Its scarlet eye, as big as a fist,
scans through the crowd of men gathered around.
A more fearsome cyclops does not exist,
wearing white bones of men he slayed upon his wrist.

His massive maw opens, a vast bellow
bursts forth, "Is there no man here who is bold
enough to accept my charge, no fellow
who thinks their might meets mine? I hold
no tricks, no deceitful lies have I told,
only seeking a soul who will wager
his life against mine. Come forward, uphold
your glorious kingdom against nature.
Grapple and spar with me, come forth into danger."

Stepping forward is she, monster huntress by trade,
red curls emblazoned by morning sun rays.
A hushed silence ensues. She draws her blade
and calls back to her foe, "Go! Run away
if you value your head or I shall slay
you where you stand. Your words may strike terror
into the hearts of these men, but today
you face a stronger soul. I am bearer
of truth. Facing me would be a fatal error."

Laughter erupts from the mouth of the beast,
that hideous cyclops towering high
above her head. He thinks she is the least
of his concerns, brushing aside her cry
to answer his challenge, wanting an ally
of noble line or some warrior man
to heed his call. She stands firm to deny
his jest, rooted in place, knowing she can
defeat this foul monster and ruin his evil plan.

"Does race of man now place their faith within

the feats of a woman? Do you mock me
now with insult, sending mother of kin
to wage your war? Not one will remain free
by end of day if this woman will be
your champion, mark down my words. Your end
will come unless man steps up. I foresee
what your future will hold, now simply send
some strapping youth among you forward to amend."

No man dares move, no courage stirs, because
of mocking words. But on that plain she cries
again, "I will be the end of your cause,
the one to break your reign. You can chastise
me all you want, but truth will shatter lies."
With sword she sprints across terrain, toward
her fearsome foe, thinking how to devise
a plan to bring the giant down, to ward
off the attack of the champion of the horde.

Canto III

She weaves between the swipes of cyclops' spear,
nimble with grace unfound in men. She stabs
its skin, striking spots exposed, keeping clear
of attempts to counter. He spins to nab
her frail form. She dives onto the drab
grass that has been trampled by goblin feet,
rolling to evade. Orc hands reach to grab
her and a cry is raised from troops to call out
their foe's craven deceit interfering the bout.

Some shallow scrapes remain behind in the wake
of claws letting her go. They crowd to press
toward her waiting foe, eager to partake
in spectacle of gore. Her eyes assess
the brute for some advantage to possess

that would even the odds, any small flaw
she can exploit. She determines success
belongs to her if she provokes to draw
out his weakness, to strikes his pride until it's raw.

She breaks from the army behind her, arms
held overhead, taunting her foe. She cries
out, hurling insults and vile names to harm
his vast ego. A sharp crimson hue dyes
his cheeks, his veins snaking up as they rise
to be exposed. Ivory froth appears
around his lips, he stammers and denies
the claims and roars for her to come stand near
and say those lies. She smirks at his response severe.

He spurs into action, rushing toward
her, spear lowered to pierce right through her chest.
His self-restraint is gone, mind in discord
with emotion. She spins away, unstressed
by his assault, moving as though possessed
by dancing warrior spirits. Her blade
strikes flesh time after time, getting the best
of the exchange. She sees pride has betrayed
him here; the realization makes her feel dismayed.

This same weakness she now exploits has been
her own downfall, her flaw she faced the day
before against the raging beast. Her sin
she sees clearly for the first time, the way
it has consumed her soul. With great dismay
she vows to change, to cast aside the pride
that could have caused her fall. Guilt fades away
with her resolve, with the changes inside
her heart she has become cleansed, the weight brushed aside.

She weathers his fierce storm of rage, the two

trading blows with weapons until the sun
begins to set. They drip sweat and blood, hew
armor with blows mighty. With each strike given
both sides react, cheering their champion.
Her sword, once light and nimble in her hands,
feels like a boulder from constant action.
Between gasping breaths she issues commands
provoking the cyclops to give in to demands.

His giant fist slams to the ground, driving
through dirt and stone. His motions are slow so she
swiftly seizes the chance she needs, diving
across the battlefield, striking gutsy
blows while running up his long arm. A sea
of red spatters the ground as she slashes
his neck and stabs his eye. She stops, dives free
from his body as he blindly thrashes,
desperately flailing as life flees from gashes.

The corpse blackens as breath departs, decay
in death reigns triumphant. Monsters all cry
in low lament, their champion today
has been beaten. They turn and flee to try
to find escape from their defeat. The sky
is dark and men around campfires rejoice
in victory, proclaim her name, and cry
out she is their savior. Within her a choice
arises: bask in pride or deny their voices.

Their jubilee carries until morning,
the men lavish her great gifts and praise
and feast in her honor. She gives warning
that they should keep their gifts, she only stays
to rest from her battle and will part ways
as soon as she is healed. Those words they heed
not, insisting to give reward for days

to come. A part of her calls to concede
to their requests, but she rises above her greed.

She mounts her horse, no rest will she find here,
and so she rides again along the road.
Fatigue threatens to plague her mind, but fear
of going back, giving in to pride, goads
her on toward the next village. The load
she bore upon her soul has now withdrawn,
mastered the past two days, those fights showed
her flaw and the problems that could feed on
her pride. Unbroken now, she rides into the dawn.

THE MONSTERS WE CREATE

BY P.A. CORNELL

"Time for school!" Paul's mom called.

Paul rose from the bed feeling a weight inside him, like an anchor trying to hold him in place. He wanted to give into it, but knew he couldn't. Mom would make him go to school no matter what. Especially knowing that he had a math test.

He grabbed some rumpled clothes from the floor, sighing as he caught his reflection in the mirror, then headed for the bathroom to finish getting ready before heading downstairs.

"Mom, why do you always buy me clothes that are like three sizes too big?" he called, taking the stairs two-at-a-time.

His mom turned to him and smiled, "Oh sweetie, they're just a little loose. But you're due for a growth spurt any day now. You'll be filling those clothes out in no time."

"The kids at school don't need any more reasons to pick on me," he argued.

She shook her head, smiling as though amused. "Those kids are nothing compared to you, Paul. Pretty soon they'll see that."

Paul sighed again, grabbing his backpack and heading for the door without bothering to have breakfast. The heavy weight filled his stomach.

Jumping the back fence, Paul headed for the wooded area that separated his house from the school property. At least none of the kids from school took the forest path. They were superstitious and talked about the monsters that stalked kids in these woods. Paul thought they were stupid. He might have been the smallest kid in the seventh grade, but at least he wasn't afraid of monsters. He knew there was no such thing. The only monsters he knew of had names like "Dan" and "Terry" and were considered the cool kids at school.

In the woods he felt free from them. He passed his favourite tree, the one with the bark that looked kind of like a smiling face. That's when he saw the monarch butterfly just up ahead.

Paul wished he had his net with him, but he'd have to make due. He unzipped his backpack with care, and removed a disposable plastic container of raw vegetables from his lunch bag. He opened it and let the vegetables drop into the bag. Then, using the fork for his pasta, he punched a few holes into the container lid.

Taking each step with the greatest care, he moved toward the butterfly. As he got closer, he managed to corner the monarch with the box, while scooping it in with the lid before snapping it shut. It was a tight squeeze for the butterfly but it could still move.

"What's that you got there?"

Paul looked up to see his next door neighbour, Mrs. Samuels, heading in the opposite direction on the path. Like Paul, the elderly woman was not superstitious and often took her daily walks through the woods.

"Hi Mrs. Samuels," he said. "I caught a butterfly. Just to look at though. I'll let it go, later."

"I know you will," she said with a smile. "Do you think you could come help me with some leaves that need raking after school?"

"Sure, Mrs. 'S'. I'll be there."

"Thank you so much Paul," she said with a smile. "I'll see if I can maybe bake you some banana muffins for your trouble."

He smiled and moved to the side to let the older woman pass. He liked Mrs. Samuels. She was always nice to him and always willing to listen when he needed to talk. Helping her with the things she had trouble with was the least he could do. In many ways, she was his only friend.

Paul threw the box with the butterfly into his backpack and continued up the path. As he emerged through the trees onto school grounds, he heard voices. Here we go again, he thought.

"Hey wimp," said Dan.

A group of kids stood around Dan, snickering. Paul tried his best to ignore them and headed right past Dan toward the school building. It was so close. Just a few more steps and he'd be inside and relatively safe. But as he passed, Dan grabbed his backpack strap and yanked it right off his shoulder.

Before Paul could reach for it, Dan had unzipped it and turned it upside down so that everything inside fell to the muddy ground.

"Oh shoot! Sorry dude," he said, laughing.

A couple of the other boys grabbed hold of Paul, while Dan made sure to stomp his things further into the mud. Then he saw Vanessa—the most popular girl in school—move toward his lunch bag.

"What have we got here?" she asked.

Reaching in, she pulled out the thermos and handed it to Dan, who unscrewed the lid and spilled spaghetti and meatballs all over the ground. Then she dumped out the vegetables. And with them the box holding the monarch.

"Whoa, what's that?" asked Terry, one of the boys holding Paul.

"Ooh, is that a pretty butterfly?" Dan mocked. He then raised his foot and stomped the plastic container into the ground, crushing the monarch inside. "Not so pretty now, is it?"

The bell rang and the other kids took off at a run, leaving Paul to pick up his muddy belongings. He didn't care about his lunch, but he felt bad for the butterfly.

"I should have just left you in the woods," he said. "All the monsters are out here anyway."

The weight in his stomach now felt something more like

heat. Like a furnace burning inside of him. It was not a new feeling. He often felt this when the other kids picked on him, but this time it felt stronger, as if the burning were fuelled by his anger over the butterfly. But what could he do? He choked it down as always, heading for class.

The day continued in the same way, for the most part. While in class he heard the others whispering "nerd" each time he answered a teacher's question. Even during the math test he caught angry glares from the corner of his eye. Once he turned in the direction of a giggle, only to catch a knowing glance between Vanessa and another girl, followed by more laughter.

Between classes, while they moved through the halls, he was shoved as other kids walked by. The girls whispered insults under their breath. One even filled her mouth with water at the fountain and spit it in his face as he walked by. He dried it hastily with his own shirtsleeve and continued on, trying to ignore everything they did. Just trying to get to the next classroom where he could pretend not to notice what they said and did around him.

Recess was a different story. There was no escape there. The teachers, more interested in their conversations than in acting as referees, pretended not to notice when other kids accidentally threw balls at his head or tripped him as he walked.

The school day dragged on, as they always did. He found himself looking forward to the time after school, raking leaves for Mrs. Samuels, and later playing videogames or just taking a nap until he was called for dinner. Sleep was his friend. It made time pass unnoticed. It took the pain away. He slept as much as he could these days.

When the final bell rang, Paul gathered his things as quickly as possible and rushed out the door. He ran for the woods like his life depended on it. Past experience had taught him that hanging around could only be bad for him.

He had nearly made it when he felt something sharp and hard hit the back of his head, followed by a warm wetness that quickly cooled in the autumn air. The shock of it knocked him to the ground just a few feet from the woods.

"Where are you off to in such a hurry, loser?" a voice asked from behind him.

Paul turned to see the popular kids heading his way, Terry in the lead. Not far from where he found himself on all fours was a bloody rock, about the size of a softball. He couldn't believe they had thrown it at him. Was there nothing they wouldn't do to him?

As Terry reached him, Paul watched almost as if outside himself as the other boy paused, pulled back his leg and kicked it with full force into his stomach. Too shocked and dazed to react, Paul felt his body react for him. His empty stomach lurched, heaving bile up and out of his body and onto the grass.

"Ew!" said Vanessa. "Don't get too close Terry. You'll ruin your shoes!"

The group laughed, then turned and headed back toward the school. It seemed that spilling two different kinds of Paul's body fluids had been enough entertainment for one afternoon.

Paul, feeling less dazed, picked himself up. Shouldering his backpack of muddy belongings, he headed toward the woods, though much more slowly than he had been. A palm placed to the back of his head told him he was still bleeding, though not too much. He'd get his mom to look at it when he got home.

Paul opened the back door. The comforting smell of whatever his mother was making for dinner filled the room. When she saw him she looked at him with a tender smile, her head tilted with concern.

"What did they do this time, baby?" she asked.

Paul said nothing, but dropped his backpack by the door, moving closer to show her his head.

"Little monsters!" his mother said. "They should be caged."

"Maybe you should call the school this time," Paul said. "I mean, they're throwing rocks now."

"Oh honey," said his mother. "Your father and I both went through this same thing when we were your age. Trust me when I tell you that getting involved will only make things worse. And like your father says, you have to learn to resolve this on your own. It's part of growing up."

She led him over to the kitchen sink where she began washing the back of his head with cool water, taking care not to hurt him. She then patted it dry with a clean dish cloth, making sure he was no longer bleeding.

"I don't think you need stitches," she told him. "Looks like the bleeding has stopped and I think you'll heal up in no time. But you might have a bit of a headache for a bit."

Paul nodded.

"Don't worry sweetheart," she said. "They'll get theirs in the end. You just hang in there. You'll see. This is just one faze in your life. One day soon they'll regret having treated you this way. I mean, you look like you've grown a bit since this morning, even!"

"Sure," Paul said, "I'm a freaking giant. I'm going next door. Mrs. Samuels needs help with some leaves."

"Sure thing," said his mother. "But don't be too long. The lasagna's almost ready, and a growing boy needs a good supper."

Paul headed out the back door again. Growing boy, he thought. I wish.

He knocked on Mrs. Samuels's back door and she opened it, releasing the incredible smell of homemade banana muffins, which she knew were his favourite. Paul's stomach growled with the anticipation of finally getting some food.

"Paul," said Mrs. Samuels with concern. "Why is your head wet?"

"It's nothing," he told her. "My mom just had to clean a cut, that's all. I'm fine. I'll just go get the rake and get started."

But as he turned to leave, she grabbed his arm.

"Come in for a second," she said. "The leaves will still be there."

Paul did as she said and let himself be led to her kitchen table where a bread basket full of muffins waited. She took one from the basket, placed it on a saucer and put it in front of him, then sat in the opposite chair.

"It's those kids from school who hurt you again, isn't it?" she said.

Paul took a bite of muffin, but nodded.

Mrs. Samuels exhaled, shaking her head. "I don't know why your parents let this go on. I never had children of my own, mind you, and far be it from me to criticize anyone, but this is getting out of hand."

"It's ok," said Paul. "I'm used to it anyway."

"Well you shouldn't have to be used to it," she said. "You are a good boy, with a good heart. I mean, you're so kind you don't even fight back. You don't deserve to be treated like this."

Paul smiled. "Thanks Mrs. 'S', but I don't fight back because they're all bigger and stronger than me. Not because I'm so nice."

"Well, still," she said. "You're a good enough person to know violence isn't the answer."

Paul finished his muffin and stood, heading back toward the door.

"I'll get those leaves done for you now," he said.

"Thanks Paul," she said. "Be sure to take home as many muffins as you like when you're finished."

"Thanks, I will."

The school year continued to go pretty much the same way for Paul. Over time, though, the bullies began to get more and more confident. They had even started to wait for him at the edge of the forest. Paul felt like they were invading his only refuge. Would there soon be nowhere left that was safe? Would they follow him all the way home one day? Would they let themselves in and continue attacking him until they finished him off? Or drove him to do it himself?

He tried not to think about it too much. For the time being, they still avoided going into the woods and he was able to dodge most of their more violent attacks at school. There wasn't much they could get away with there anyway since, by law, the teachers could only let things go so far.

Even though the bullying had gotten worse, though, Paul's parents still refused to get involved.

"Can't you guys do something to help me?" he asked one day.

"Son, these experiences help you grow," his father told him. "It's like they say, 'what doesn't kill you makes you stronger'."

"Yes," said his mother. "And look how much you've grown already this year."

Paul shook his head and held back the tears, pushing it all down inside that furnace in his stomach. They just didn't get it.

He let the feelings burn inside the imaginary furnace, but it seemed like they were never fully burned away. As numb as he felt when he pushed them down, he knew they were in there, bubbling at the pit of his stomach. Like a volcano waiting to erupt. He wondered what would happen if it ever did.

Paul was spending more and more time at Mrs. Samuels's house. She was the only one who seemed to care what was going on. Paul told her how his parents refused to get involved and insisted this would pass. She didn't say much in return, but he could tell she didn't agree with them.

Mrs. "S" was like having a grandmother he could go to. She was always willing to listen. And while he was there he would find things to help her with.

She was the only person in his life who seemed to see him as a real person. A good person. He knew she valued his friendship too.

"Paul, how have things been going with those bullies at school?" she asked.

"The same," he said, looking down at the dishes he was washing.

"I know it's not my place to get involved," she said. "But would you like me to go to the school and talk to the principal?"

Paul looked at her. He felt such gratitude for what she was trying to do, but he also knew her help would only make things worse for him. And chances were the principal wouldn't take her seriously since she wasn't even a family member.

"Thanks," said Paul. "I think it's better if you don't though. They would pick on me more if they knew that you and me were... I mean that we spend time together."

"That you're friends with an old lady, you mean," she said with a laugh. "I understand."

"My parents say this is just part of growing up," said Paul. "That they went through it too."

"Well, not everyone does," she replied. "But I hope that if you must go through this, that you don't let it make you bitter. That I still see this sweet boy when I look at the man you'll become." She pinched his cheek lightly enough not to hurt him and they both smiled.

"I'm glad I at least have you to talk to," said Paul.

"Me too," she said.

"Time for school!"

Paul felt his eyes snap open. He'd been dreaming something

44

horrible about big, hairy monsters. A dream that made him feel like a pathetic little kid. No wonder they picked on him.

Paul turned on his iPad and checked Facebook. Someone had hacked his account and posted a picture of him in his underwear, changing after gym class. He deleted it, and changed his password and privacy settings for the second time that year.

As he showered, he imagined he was washing off the humiliation. He tried to visualize it sliding down the drain, gone forever. But the burning in his stomach told him it was far from over.

He dressed, noticing that his pants seemed less bagged around the ankles than they had been yesterday. The waist fit a little more snug. His shirt, too, sagged less in the shoulders and his chest seemed to fill the fabric a bit more closely. "That's impossible," he told his reflection. "I think mom constantly telling me I've grown is starting to get to me."

His doubts were confirmed at school when no one seemed to notice he was any bigger either. He was still smaller and weaker than the rest of them and they made sure to never let him forget it.

But then something even stranger than imaginary overnight growth happened. In class, Vanessa sent him a text.

Paul's first thought was to just ignore it, but he couldn't help but glance at the first part. The words said, "Paul, I'm so sorry."

He had to read it again to make sure he wasn't seeing things, and then continued reading to see if it was just the setup to something along the lines of, "I'm so sorry you're such a loser."

"I saw the pic of u on Fb this A.M. I feel so bad. I know I've been mean 2, but this really made me see things differently. I wish I was strong enough 2 stand up to everyone, but I'm not like u. I couldn't take getting picked on."

Paul stopped and glanced up at Vanessa. She was staring

straight ahead at the teacher, but then shifted her eyes for just a second in his direction.

He continued reading. "I'd like 2 be your secret friend if that's cool. We could walk home from school today. But I don't want the others 2 know. K?"

Paul wasn't sure what to do. But she sounded so sincere. Plus she was so pretty. "K," he texted back.

He looked up at Vanessa again. She didn't look at him but he saw her check her phone, then smile.

Paul felt a different sort of warmth inside him. It spread out from his chest and seemed to fill his whole body. He could almost feel his skin tingling. He couldn't help but stare at her for the rest of the day. He hadn't really thought about how pretty she was when she'd been mean to him. Sure, he couldn't say he hadn't noticed, but he had pushed away those feelings along with all the others. Now they had been freed and he caught himself thinking about the walk home after school. What would they talk about? What would happen if the others saw? He could never let them hurt her like they'd hurt him. He'd protect her somehow if it came to that.

He felt happy for the first time in ages. Even when other kids picked on him later in the day, he didn't let it bother him. He thought only of the walk home. How he would show Vanessa the best path. The tree that looked like it had a face on its trunk. Maybe one day he'd even bring her over to meet Mrs. Samuels. By the time the final bell rang, Paul was all but singing to himself.

For Vanessa's sake, he was careful heading for the woods this time, not wanting to be followed. But for once it seemed luck was on his side.

When he reached the woods he found Vanessa waiting just behind the first few trees so that no one would see her.

"Hi," he said, out of breath with excitement.

She smiled. "Hi Paul. Ready to go?"

Paul nodded and took the lead, following the path he knew so well he could have walked it with his eyes closed. Vanessa followed, her voice sounding a little nervous to be going this deep into the woods, but she chatted all the same about school assignments, a sleepover coming up at a friend's house, and other everyday things.

Paul didn't say much, but he listened, enjoying the sound of her voice, so different now that she wasn't being mean. It was hard to see her as the same girl who not so long ago had dumped out his lunch bag.

Lost in these thoughts, he didn't notice at first when she stopped. He turned to see her standing a few feet behind him on the path, an odd look on her face.

"Don't worry," he told her. "We're almost half way through. There's a tree just up ahead that has these knobby bumps on the trunk that kind of look like a face. Come on, I'll show you."

She smiled then, and he couldn't help but smile back. But then something in her smile changed and without knowing why, he felt a chill in that place in his chest where he'd been so warm earlier that day. A familiar tight knot began to form in his stomach.

"It's about time you got here, loser."

Paul turned and saw Dan and Terry blocking the path in front of them. His first thought was to protect Vanessa, but when he turned to reassure her, he saw the old, familiar smirk on her face. She's just playing along with them, he told himself. She's just scared. But as the punches and kicks began to land, he had no choice but to accept the truth. She had tricked him. It had all been a lie. She had gotten him to drop his guard just so they could hurt him, and here of all places. The woods were no longer his.

He didn't know how much time passed, but when they finally got tired of kicking him, they stopped. Then Vanessa kicked mud in his face and they began walking back in the direction of the school. Paul lay there on the path listening to the voices get quieter until all he could hear was the sound of his own breathing.

It took more effort than he had expected to get himself up

on all fours. He didn't bother trying to stand, but crawled the rest of the way home. As low to the ground as his mood.

When he arrived home, his mother saw him through the window and met him at the back gate. Mrs. Samuels, who'd been watering her rose bush in her back yard, walked over and joined them. Together they helped him up and led him into the house. There he cried in spite of himself, feeling as though he were growing smaller, no matter what his mom told him.

"Look at him," said Mrs. Samuels. "Look at what these kids have done to him. Enough is enough. You need to tell the school."

"Thank you Mrs. Samuels. I'll take it from here," said his mother. She all but pushed the older woman out the door, then shut it behind her. "Poor thing," she said to Paul. "Looks like you've had a rougher day than most. That's the thing about kids. They come into this world so innocent and pure, but as they grow they are capable of such cruelty. What they don't see is that with every vicious act they take a piece of that pure soul and use it to feed the monster." She smiled at this part, which seemed strange to Paul.

He wasn't sure what she had meant by all that, but he didn't care. He dragged himself upstairs and lay down without even bothering to clean himself up. Then he slept until morning, having no idea if his mother had even called him for supper.

As he showered and washed off the blood and dirt, Paul noticed each sore muscle, feeling his ribs with care. He had expected broken bones but was surprised to find none. It seemed he was made from tougher stuff than he'd thought.

He dressed, noticing the bruises in the mirror. But he also noticed something strange. His clothes fit. This time he was sure of it. Yesterday they had still been a little loose, but now they fit perfectly. He actually looked kind of good.

Running downstairs, he stopped to grab a piece of toast before heading out the door. He was in such a rush he barely paused to nod to his parents. They said nothing, but as the door slammed shut behind him he could have sworn he heard his father say, "I think he's nearly ready."

Paul felt strange. He had expected to feel sore and broken today. He had gone over in his head how he would convince his parents to let him stay home from school, but something was pulling him there instead. He hopped the back fence with greater ease than ever. The weight in his stomach was gone, replaced by a lightness that warmed him almost as yesterday's short-lived joy had. He felt confident for the first time in his life. Whatever those jerks had in store for him today, he would face it head-on. He would not hide.

"Paul!" called Mrs. Samuels from her yard.

Despite his haste, Paul stopped and waited for the old woman to reach her gate.

"Paul," she said again. "Are you sure you'll be alright walking to school on your own? I can go with you if you like."

Paul smiled. "I appreciate it Mrs. 'S', but I'll be fine. Really. You don't need to worry about me."

She gave him a strange look, but Paul didn't have time to figure out the mind of an old lady. He gave her a quick wave and headed off toward the trees.

As he reached the centre of the woods, he began to hear laughter. But he had expected this. Now that the woods didn't scare them anymore, they would be waiting. They would always be waiting. But he would not let them have this place.

He almost ran to them when he saw them. Vanessa was snickering as Dan and Terry came closer to start the fresh beating. Dan landed the first punch. It was strong and hit Paul square in the face, but he stood his ground. Then Terry shoved him. Paul stepped back but he didn't fall.

Vanessa still laughed, but she seemed less sure now as the boys continued their attack and Paul continued to take it.

Paul felt his stomach grow warm again, and that warmth spread through his body. It was pure rage that filled him and he let it. He no longer pushed it down, he set it free. The volcano was erupting. He felt his whole body change then. The warmth moved into his limbs and he felt himself stronger. His skin began to almost glow as the heat reached his face and then he felt the anger pour out his eyes.

Vanessa stopped laughing, and he saw pure terror bleach the colour from her face. She looked like she was about to run, but then something seemed to stop her, and she just stood there, tears streaming down her cheeks.

The boys also stood where they were, shocked and speechless until Dan said, "Jesus Christ! What are you?"

Paul took hold of Dan's shoulders. He had imagined that he would start to hit Dan back, but instead he just held the other boy. Not with any real effort, as Dan seemed frozen, but just enough as if to hold him steady. Enough for Paul to focus on him. Then he felt a powerful surge fill him. He could see something draining out of Dan and feel it entering him. He couldn't stop himself, nor did he want to. He let the feeling fill his body, getting ever stronger. Watching Dan get weaker. Then the feeling stopped and he let Dan go, the boy's lifeless body dropping to the ground.

Paul didn't know why the others didn't run. Maybe they couldn't. Maybe he was somehow keeping them there. It didn't matter. He moved to Terry next, repeating the process. Feeling himself grow stronger as the other boy grew weaker. This was it, he thought. This was what mom meant when she talked about kids feeding the monster with their cruelty.

Having finished with Terry, he moved to Vanessa. He no longer felt the urgency he had when he'd first found them in the woods, so he took his time with her. He held her almost gently, tears still streaming from her eyes though she made no sound. It was like a rich dessert after a feast, meant to be savoured.

When he finished, he lay her down on the path next to the boys. He stood tall, looking down on them for a moment. They couldn't hurt him now. Sure, the school had plenty of bullies left, but he knew he could handle them.

He noticed how much larger and stronger he was now. Like the pictures he'd seen of his father when he was younger. Lean yet muscular. Powerful.

"Paul... what did you do?"

He turned to see Mrs. Samuels, standing on the path just behind him. Her eyes were glued to the other kids, her mouth open in what looked almost like a soundless scream. Then her eyes shifted to Paul's and she took a step back. Then another, nearly bumping into a tree. Her face went a sickly pale colour.

"No," she said. Then she turned and ran as fast as her old legs could carry her, stumbling as she went.

"Mrs. Samuels!" Paul called after her. He started running too, but soon stopped. What did it matter anyway? He didn't need her anymore. "Well no one told you to follow me anyway!" he yelled.

Instead of heading to his neighbour's, Paul went home. He walked through the door, somehow knowing that his parents would be expecting him. As he stepped into the living room he found them sipping their morning coffees. They looked up at him and smiled.

"See sweetie," his mother said, "I told you you'd fill those clothes up soon enough."

His dad patted him on his shoulder.

"I'm proud of you son," he said. "I knew you'd be able to handle this on your own. And look how much stronger you are for it."

"You two went through this too," said Paul. "This... change."

"Like a butterfly," his mom said. "It's what happens to our kind at this age. The age at which human children are often the cruelest. Their anger and hatred feeds us. So we become our true selves."

Paul thought of the monarch butterfly crushed to death in his plastic container. For the first time since it had happened he could picture it without cringing. Without sadness. Without feeling anything, really. He wondered why such a pathetic creature had even mattered to him in the first place.

"Mrs. Samuels saw," he said.

"Don't worry about her," mom said, "We'll handle her."

"Now get your things together son," said his dad. "This is just the beginning. You have a big day ahead of you. Lots of bullies left."

"That's right," said his mom. "Time for school."

NATURAL SELECTION

BY TONI J. LYNCH-BRADISH

Running his hand through his hair, the man paced around the chair in front of him like a predator stalking its prey. The silence in the room became too much and he finally lowered his head in defeat and walked to the chair to sit. With his head still bowed he tried to collect his thoughts. His decision to look up instantly filled him with regret as he stared into the sad tired eyes across from him.

Breaking the hypnotic gaze he looked to one side of the room.

"We can't go on like this," he mumbled.

"We're just not happy. We tried, but only just barely. We've been faking it at best. I think we were happy for a short time but..."

He met the eyes across from him again and sighed heavily.

"We smile... we've gotten very good at smiling... but we've been faking it for years."

The man shifted guiltily under the unwavering stare from the eyes across from him.

"You think it's all my fault don't you? Maybe it is. I don't know why I do it. It's like there's a beast inside me; a monstrous dictator that controls my every move. I tried therapy, you know that. You know I did! I felt like I was suffocating in that place, surrounded by broken souls in various stages of mending and unraveling."

He shut his eyes tight and tried to block out the memories of his sessions. The more he tried to forget, though, the more he could see the judging expression on the face of his appointed therapist. Clearly it was his fault the therapy didn't work. The sessions were supposed to heal him but they didn't. To him that meant he was irreparable.

He looked up at the face across from him and the unapologetic, judging eyes were all too familiar. Unable to sit still any longer he jumped out of his seat and began to pace again. He couldn't exactly pinpoint which emotion was stronger at that moment; the anger or the loneliness. His face was flushed and his hands began to shake. The frustration of it was almost too much. The therapy had always left him feeling lonely and unsupported but who could he trust enough to share those feelings? Anger and blame were so much easier to unleash.

"Say something... You never say anything! Why don't you help? This is as much your fault as it is mine!"

The eyes across from him were difficult to read; a mixture of emotions contorted the face as the man tried to steady himself on back of the chair. They were both in so much pain. His anger started to ebb as the sadness started to take over again. He could feel the tears streaming down his face before he even realized he was crying. The rollercoaster course his emotions were on began to wear him out.

"I've become so broken that it's physical... it is more than sadness, it affects my whole body. Can't you see?" He slowly sat back down in the chair. Not bothering to brush away the tears on his cheeks, he pleaded.

"I'm always exhausted. At times, I can barely focus on even the most mundane tasks because of my racing thoughts and I just shut down. I interact with the people around me as if I'm on autopilot. Responding with whatever sounds appropriate without giving it much thought." He looked up at the ceiling trying to steady his voice. Taking a deep breath, he continued.

"I move through each day just to get closer to death so it all will be over sooner."

He waved his hand dismissively and looked back down at his feet, avoiding the person across from him. "Reminds me of a movie I saw once about a man with a magical remote control fast forwarding through his life."

A barely audible chuckle from across the room made him look up with a grim expression on his face.

"How can you still find it in yourself to laugh? You don't deserve even a moment of happiness. You're a monster, you hurt people... you hurt me."

He started to get up and walk away again but was suddenly filled with overwhelming rage and spun around to face the sad accusing eyes once more. They almost made him pause but he knew one of them had to go and had decided at just that moment, he wanted to live again not just merely be alive.

He dashed across the space between them until they were practically nose-to-nose. The man that was him. The man that represented everything he hated about himself. He stood for a moment in front of the mirror and continued to speak to himself.

"It's time for you to go. We can't go on like this. Not with both of us. We've been together a long time. Too long. Too much of my life."

The memories flooded in; the lost jobs, the broken relationships, the isolation, the last few decades of unhappiness; memory after memory until he felt like he was drowning and the need to save himself consumed him.

A screamed erupted from his throat that was barely recognizable as human as he threw his body against the mirror. He fell, got up, and rushed at it again and again with his entire body. He kicked, he punched, he charged at it with every ounce of strength in him, not caring about the pain or the blood.

"I won't let you kill me!" he slammed his fists into the mirror repeatedly until he was pounding on nothing but the wooden back and the frame. He was surrounded by silence as the echoes of his screams died down and he surveyed the damage he had done. The reflection was gone and there was just plain wood there now. There was no one in the room except him now. He collapsed to the floor and began to laugh and cry at the same time.

"He's gone," looking down at his battered hands, "but I'm finally here"

GAIT

BY C. P. ROELKE

I saw him coming from two blocks away, and could tell by the way he was walking that today was one of his bad days. As I sat on the bus stop bench, watching him continue to get closer, like a storm cloud rolling in, I contemplated running a block over and taking a different bus home. That would only hurt his feelings, though, making it worse the next time, so I sat there and waited for him.

"Hey Paul, saltines today," I said as he reached the bench, offering him a sleeve of crackers I had pulled out of my backpack. He dropped a plastic grocery bag on the ground near the edge of the bench without saying a word, glaring at me. The bag made a heavy clinking sound when it hit the pavement.

"They'll be right here if you want them," I said, placing the crackers on the edge of the bench.

Paul began pacing back and forth in front of the bench as he continued to glare at me. He blew out loud, angry breaths, his nostrils flaring like a bull's in one of those old cartoons. This was real though, and much more frightening. Being as discreet as possible, I slid my pocketknife out of my pants and into my jacket pocket, flipping it open. I gripped it tightly; my muscles tensed for action, and tracked Paul's movements with my eyes.

Paul continued to pace back and forth for several minutes,

then walked over to his bag and reached into it without taking his eyes off me. He pulled a tallboy can of some cheap beer out of the bag, cracked it open, and sucked the foam off the top before returning to his pacing. Every once in a while he would turn towards the cars zooming past on their evening commute, spread his arms wide, and beat a fist against his chest, as if inviting them to come after him. I sat there and watched him for several minutes, but it felt like hours, my muscles tiring from their prolonged tension, until he walked back over to the bench.

Smacking the crackers out of his way, Paul plopped down next to me and eyed me for a few moments, sipping his beer. I stared at the sidewalk and watched him out of my peripheral vision, not wanting to upset him more by looking into his eyes. As we sat there in silence, I noticed an odd odour, aside from his normal homeless man stench, emanating from him. It smelled metallic. Venturing a quick glance at Paul, I saw that blood had begun to drip out of his nose, soaking into the matted hair of his beard.

"Paul, your nose is bleeding," I said, locking eyes with him. With a sudden flick of his wrist, he swiped under his nose, leaving a red streak on the back of his hand.

"Who told you my name?" He asked me in an accusatory tone.

"You did. We met last month, I'm Mark. Me and you sit and talk at this bus stop most days. I always bring you some food, remember?" I answered in as calm a voice as I could muster. Paul stared at me for several seconds, still looking angry, but I could see his mind churning behind his eyes.

"Oh," he said after a pregnant pause and took a long swig of his beer. He continued to contemplate what I had told him for another minute before tilting the mouth of his beer towards me. "Want some beer?"

"No thanks."

"What did you bring to eat?"

"Saltines," I said, pointing to where they lay on the ground. Paul glanced down at the package of crackers.

"Fuck 'em," he grunted and took another pull from the can, staring off across the road, visibly preoccupied.

"Something on your mind, Paul?" I ventured, hoping he was lucid and sober enough to have a conversation. He shot me a suspicious look, his eyes narrow.

"Why?" He asked, his anger beginning to mount again.

"You just seemed to be lost in thought, what's up?" I asked, giving him an earnest look, trying to mask my agitation. Paul got that distant look in his eyes again before he spoke.

"Last night I was down the way," he said, pointing down the road towards the bluffs in the distance, "having myself a beer in Wichita Park."

"Do you go down there often?" I interjected. A few goose bumps rose on my arms at the mention of Wichita Park. The park was across the street from my apartment, I hoped he had not followed me home one night. I do not how he could have without me noticing, as he would have had to ride my bus, but you never know.

"Not so much, I was over looking for my friend. I walked down there because I hadn't seen him around for some time. I found his tent, but he wasn't inside, so I sat down to have my beer. That's when I saw the eyes."

"Eyes?"

"Cat's eyes, but too big for a cat, glowing golden through the blackness. Witch's eyes."

"You saw a witch?"

"I just told you, I saw her eyes... and her eyes saw mine..." Paul quieted and stared off across the road again, his beer forgotten.

"What did you do?"

"Nothing. I tried to run, but I was rooted to the ground like a tree," he answered, continuing to stare off at nothing, "her gaze held me down. She put me into a trance, time like ages passed, and I woke up to the light of an unnatural fire and I was surrounded by devils. More time went by and I woke again, shivering cold. Some angels stood over me and put a blanket on me. I woke once more and it was daylight. I was in my friend's tent, but he was still gone."

"Oh. Well... I'm glad you eventually got away," I responded, coming to the conclusion that he was far from sober. Paul grunted and chugged the remainder of his beer. Standing up, he pitched the empty can into the gutter, grabbed his bag, and strode out into the street without checking for traffic. Tires screeched as a car, blaring its horn, skidded to stop just inches from Paul. He flipped the driver off and disappeared behind a building on the other side of the road.

When he was out of sight, I closed my knife, but left it in my jacket pocket, and stood up. Picking up Paul's beer and my package of broken crackers, I tossed them in a garbage can and sat back down to continue waiting. A few minutes later another couple of homeless people, a man and a woman, approached and sat down on another nearby bench. The woman put a cigarette between her lips, lit it, took a long drag, and held it out to the man, who sat hunched over glaring at the sidewalk. He snatched it out of her hand, took a couple quick puffs, and thrust it back in front of her face, all without taking his eyes off the sidewalk.

The wail of a car horn pulled me away from my people watching and I looked up at the street. Paul was crossing the street towards the bus stop again. He walked up to the woman with the cigarette and pulled another beer out of his bag.

"Want to buy a beer?" He asked her.

"Yeah, how much?" She replied, slipping a few bills out of her pocket.

"Two dollars."

She peeled two singles off the stack and exchanged them for the beer. "Thanks," she said, cracked the can open, took a swig, and offered it to the man sitting next to her.

"I don't want that shit," he snapped, spitting on the ground.

Paul carried the two dollars into a small liquor store behind the bus stop and walked out holding two shooters of vodka just as my bus rolled up. Grabbing my backpack, I stepped onto the bus, swiped my pass, and sat down. A few seconds later, Paul walked onto the bus. He and the bus driver exchanged words, but I could not hear what was said over the hum of the bus's engine, then Paul gave me a lingering glance and stepped out onto the sidewalk. The bus driver closed the door and pulled away from the curb.

When the bus reached my stop, I got off and walked the half-mile to my apartment. As I walked in the door, my girlfriend, Lena, greeted me with a kiss.

"Hey babe, how was your day?" I asked her.

"Long. Glad it's the weekend. What about you?"

"Alright. I think Paul tried to follow me home tonight."

"That's your homeless Indian friend, yes?"

"Native, not Indian, but yes, that's Paul."

"Why would he want to follow you?"

"Beats me, he's not all there, who knows what goes through his head. He was drunk. So where do you want to go tonight?"

"I was thinking the 'Quod, is that okay?"

"If that's what you want. I'll go wherever, you pick."

"Let's go to the 'Quod then."

We left the apartment and walked through the gathering late-autumn darkness to the Pequod. Known locally as the 'Quod, it was a cozy nautical themed pub with a small reading and board game area in the back. Sitting down in a pair of big, comfy chairs, we ordered drinks and appetizers, and set up a game of checkers.

Just shy of midnight, and about five drinks in, we paid our tab and began to stumble home. As we staggered down the sidewalk that bordered Wichita Park, laughing at our drunken jokes and falling over each other, someone leaped out of some brush and crashed to the ground at our feet. Lena, frightened, screamed directly into my ear, making it ring. The person lay motionless before us, face down on the concrete. I let go of Lena and squatted next to the person.

"Hey you okay," I slurred, shaking them by the shoulder, "do you need help?"

They moaned, beginning to stir.

"Let me help you up," I said and grabbed them by the arm, pulling them to their feet.

"Mark?" I knew that voice.

"Paul? What are you doing?"

"She's after me," Paul said hurriedly, his voice rising.

"Who's after you?"

"That cat-eyed witch, she found me again. She chased me through the park."

"Witch?" Lena asked. Paul let out a yelp of surprise.

"Witch, run!"

"She's not a witch, Paul, this is my girlfriend," I explained, thinking I could reason with him in my drunken state.

"I have to be sure," he muttered under his breath and grabbed her by the hair, yanking her head back. She screamed again, this time in pain. Paul stared into her eyes for a long moment before releasing her. "Not a witch."

"Not yet, asshole, but I'm damn sure close to showing you what one looks like," Lena responded, running her fingers through her hair. An awkward silence fell between us. That's when I heard it.

"Paaaauuuuu."

Rising up from somewhere just beyond the edge of the park, we heard a long, eerie cry. It sounded like a drawn out wail, but unnatural, as if something inhuman were trying to call out to Paul.

"It's her, run!" Paul shrieked and took off running. Freaked out, I snatched Lena's hand, and sprinted after Paul. Something crashed along through the brush, keeping pace with us. We overtook Paul and turned into the parking lot of our apartment complex. Lena stumbled and fell to her knees, being dragged along for a few feet until I realized what happened. I pulled her back to her feet and we dashed across the parking lot, stopping in front of the building's outer door. I dug my keys out of my pocket and fumbled around to find the correct one. Footsteps pounded behind us, moving rapidly closer.

"Hurry!" Lena said, her voice tinged with desperation. The

keys fell out of my hand, hitting the ground with a smack. I squatted down, picked them up, isolated the correct key, and jammed it into the lock. Yanking the door open, I shoved Lena inside and stumbled in after her, slamming the door behind us. A split-second later someone, or something, crashed into the door with a heavy thud, rattling the walls. Lena screamed and clung to my arm.

"No," Paul cried from the other side of the door, slamming his fists against it repeatedly, "she's coming. Let me in. Please Mark."

I took a step forward, but Lena pulled me back.

"Don't."

"We can't just leave him, Lena, something's out there."

"Well we can't let him in here, he's a stranger."

"Not completely, I know him."

"Close enough, besides, he's sick in the head. He's not coming in here."

"I'm not leaving him to fend for himself," I said and wrestled out of her grasp.

"Don't you dare let him in."

"Shh," I said in a hushed voice, stopping in my tracks and raising my hand to quiet her.

"Did you just shush..." she began to ask, but I cut her off.

"Would you just shut up for one damn minute?" I snapped, knowing I would pay for it later, but my drunken, terrified self did not care. While we argued, the noise from outside had died down.

"He stopped."

"Do you think he's gone?"

"Don't know." I pressed my ear against the door, listening for the slightest sound. As soon as I did, something slammed into the door, hard, knocking me to the ground. The door began to rattle violently and Paul let out the most frightful scream I had ever heard, a cry of pure, abject terror.

"Ugh, what's that smell?" Lena asked as I pushed myself to my feet. That odd metallic odour I smelled earlier in the day permeated the air, but many times stronger. It was almost unbearable. Somewhere in the building a dog started to bark. Footsteps thundered above us as a pair of neighbours, an elderly woman and a twenty-something man, presumably her son, hurried down the stairs.

"What the hell's all this racket?" The old woman asked, shooting me an accusatory look, as if I was responsible for the noise.

"Why don't you go out there and find out for yourself?" Lena muttered under her breath.

"What was that? Speak up," the old woman said, turning her ear toward Lena.

"I... we... someone is being attacked out there," I interjected, sensing an argument brewing and wanting to stop it.

"Huh. Likely one of your buddies on some sort of stoner trip. You young people are all the same; godless, drug-addled heathens."

My jaw dropped, stunned. Before I could formulate a response, a siren chirped outside, and blue and red lights flickered through the cracks in the door. Another neighbour came down the steps with his cell phone pressed against his ear.

"Yep, I'm opening it right now," he said as he pushed past us without a glance and opened the door. A police officer stepped into the entryway, letting the door close behind him.

"We've taken him into custody," the officer said as the middle-aged man slipped his phone into his pocket, "do you know him?"

"They do," the old woman jumped in, pointing a bony finger at Lena and me.

"You do?"

"He's... I... we were," I replied, unable to figure out where to start.

"Okay, wait right here," the officer commanded, cutting me off, and then mumbled something into his radio. He stepped over to the door, pushed it open, and another officer walked in, holding Paul by the arm. Paul's hands were cuffed behind his back and he was bleeding from a laceration across his cheekbone.

"Do you know this man?" the first officer asked again, giving me a hard look.

"He does. I saw them drinking together at a bus stop when my son was driving me to the drug store this afternoon," the old woman said, sticking her nose in again.

"Is this true?" The officer asked me.

"He was drinking, I was just waiting for my bus."

"So you do know him."

"Sort of. He's just some guy I've talked to while waiting for the bus."

"Okay, I need you to come with us, please, sir."

"You're arresting him?" Lena asked, disbelief tingeing her voice.

"No ma'am, we just want to ask him some questions out by the car," the officer explained and beckoned to me with his hand, "if you don't mind, sir, follow us, please."

I followed the two officers out the front door. They placed Paul in the back seat of a squad car and began to ask me questions about what was going on. As my buzz wore off and a headache set in, I explained the situation and how I had come to know Paul. After about twenty minutes, the officers drove away with Paul and I headed back into the building. Lena stood there waiting for me, alone, a worried look on her face.

"Show's over," I said, "they took him to spend the night in the drunk tank. The neighbours lost interest, huh?"

"Guess so. Can you believe that busybody bitch?" Lena asked, visibly incensed.

"Really, that's what you're worried about, some crazy old wingbat?"

"There's no need to talk to me like that," she said quietly, tears beginning to well up in her eyes, "of course I'm worried, but I don't want to think about it. It was terrifying."

I wrapped my arms around her and pulled her in tight. She pinned her face against my chest and wept.

"Come on, let's go up to bed, it's been a long night," I

whispered into her ear.

"Okay," she replied with a sniff and pulled away. We went up to our apartment and, while Lena brushed her teeth in the bathroom, I tossed my keys and wallet on my nightstand and was so exhausted I collapsed face-first onto our bed. I fell asleep before Lena got out of the bathroom.

I woke up a little past noon, more fatigued than when I went to bed. A hangover had set in, leaving me with a throbbing headache. Lena lay next to me, still sound asleep, dead to the world. Walking out to the kitchen, I chugged two large glasses of water, and scarfed down a banana. Being as quiet as possible, I returned to the bedroom, slipped on my running clothes, and went out to the living room to do some stretches. When I had loosened up, I left the apartment and hit the trails in Wichita Park to try to run off my hangover and all the built up tension from the night before.

The first mile was horrendous; the pounding of my feet against the ground made my headache ten times worse, but halfway through the second mile the endorphins began to kick in. Those, combined with the crisp autumn air, began to work the pain away. Nearing my third mile, I topped a hill and slowed at what I saw at the bottom. A man stood at the base of the hill staring off into the trees, his back turned to me. He looked a lot like Paul, but I could not be certain without seeing his face. He might have just been another homeless Native that looked like Paul; sometimes it was hard to tell them apart.

I crossed to the opposite side of the trail and jogged slowly by, watching him out of the corner of my eye, trying to get a look at his face. As I neared him I began to smell a metallic odour on the air. My heartbeat quickened at the smell; it was the same scent from last night. I stopped and leaned around until I could see the man's face. It was Paul. Blood trickled from his hairline, dripping into his eyes and beard, but he did not seem to notice. He just stood there and stared off into the trees, so still I could not even see him breathing.

"Paul... you okay?" I asked, taking a couple steps toward him. His head whipped around so fast I heard his neck crack. We locked eyes. His eyes had a golden hue to them that they did not have the day before. He opened his mouth wide, to the point I thought he had dislocated his jaw, and emitted a sound I had never heard a human make; some sort of eerie howl. Shuffling forward, he swiped at me with his long, filthy nails. Flinching back, I tried to dodge the strike, but I was too slow and one of his nails sliced into my lower lip, removing a sizeable chunk. Instantly it began to bleed freely, flowing hot down my chin. Paul swiped at me again, but I smacked his hand out of the air and back-pedalled before the blow landed. Turning around, I sprinted back up the hill. When I reached the top, I ventured a quick glance over my shoulder.

Paul chased after me, but his movements were slow and jerky, like he was trying to figure out how to move inside his own skin for the first time. Continuing to run as fast as my legs would carry me, I pounded down the trail towards the edge of the park. The sound of Paul's footsteps faded behind me, but as the edge of the park came into view, I heard a loud, repeated slapping that moved rapidly closer. An instant later, Paul appeared at my side, loping along on all -fours, giving me a crazed grin.

Quick as a lightning strike, he dove at my feet, tripping me up. I crashed to the ground in a heap, cracking my skull against the paved trail. My vision went black for a moment and a rushing sound filled my ears, then something moved between my legs and I came to. Paul disentangled himself from my legs and scurried up onto my chest, clawing repeatedly at my face and neck, tearing away flaps of skin with his disgusting nails. I swung a fist at the side of his head, but he leaped sideways an instant before the blow struck, landing on his hands and knees. Hopping to my feet, I aimed a kick at his ribs, but as soon as I was upright everything spun and I lost my balance. My kick missed badly, grazing his jaw instead. He let out that creepy howl again and scuttled off into the trees.

I crashed to my knees, skinning them, and vomited into the grass. Taking a few seconds to regain my senses, I continued to kneel there, breathing heavily. When the world stopped spinning, I pushed myself back to my feet and walked home, covered in blood and woozy. When I walked into the apartment I found Lena sitting on the couch, wrapped in a blanket and playing on her phone. As the door closed itself behind me, she looked up.

"Oh god, what happened to you?" She gasped, jumping to her feet.

"Ran into Paul again," I replied. As I spoke I felt dried blood flake off my skin.

"He did this to you? I can't believe they let that psychopath out already. I'm calling down to that district and giving the sergeant a reaming. You should go to the hospital, I'll call a cab," she rambled quickly, obviously upset.

"Stop," I said, holding up a hand, "I'm not going to the hospital."

"But what if he has AIDS or hepatitis or something. Your eyes look glazed too. Did you hit your head? You could have a concussion, you need to get checked out."

"Lena. Enough," I shouted over her, stifling her chatter, "you're stressing me out. Yes, I probably have a mild concussion, but they can't do anything about it at the hospital. I'm not going, it's a waste of time."

"There's no need to yell at me," she said, sniffling, "I talk a lot when I'm scared."

"I know, I'm sorry, I'm just really freaked out. I shouldn't have yelled at you."

She wrapped herself around me and we stood there in silence, hugging, for several minutes. As we hugged, it really set in; Paul tried to kill me. I let go of Lena, hurried into the bathroom, slammed the toilet lid open and vomited again.

"Please can we go to the hospital?" Lena asked, peering around the doorframe.

"No."

"Are you at least going to make a police report?"

"No."

"Fine, whatever," she said huffily and stormed back to the couch. I wiped my mouth and flushed the toilet. Closing the bathroom door, I took a long, hot shower. When I had dried off and changed clothes, I sat down next to Lena.

"Want to order some food?" I asked her, suddenly ravenously hungry. She did not respond, just continued to stare at her phone. "Really, you're not talking to me just because I didn't go to the hospital? It's my body, Lena. They wouldn't have done anything anyway."

She snorted but did not look up from her phone.

"Fine, be that way," I said, then muttered to myself, "such bullshit."

We passed the rest of the night without speaking. Around midnight Lena went to bed, but I stayed up playing video games, afraid to go to sleep because of the concussion. An hour later our dog, Boba, walked out of the bedroom and scratched at the patio door, wanting to go outside.

"Just a minute, bud," I said, paused my game, and walked to the closet by the front door. Grabbing my jacket, I put it on, then popped open a small coffee can I kept hidden from Lena and pulled a cigarillo out of it. She hated smoking.

"Alright, let's go," I said to Boba as I crossed to the patio door and slid it open. He sauntered off into the darkness and I lit my cigarillo. Taking a long drag, I exhaled the smoke slowly and gazed up at the stars. A few moments later I heard a low growl. Dropping my gaze to the yard, I called the dog, but saw no movement. For the fourth time in two days I smelled that metallic odour again, but this time it was faint.

"Boba. Heel," I shouted, then slipped two fingers between my lips and whistled. A bush a few feet away rustled.

"Bohhhhhhhbaaa," something cried from the bush. Goosebumps crawled across my skin; I had heard that sound before.

"Boba, inside. Now," I called and the bush rustled again. I heard a yelp and Boba shot past me into the apartment. Dropping my smoke, I followed him and quickly slid the patio door shut, locked it, and closed the blinds. A second later I heard a light strumming on the door, like someone was tapping their fingernail against the glass. I considered cracking the blinds to see what was out there, but I was too creeped out, so I stood there and listened. The noise ceased a moment later and I exhaled deeply, realizing I had been holding my breath.

"Let's go to bed," I said, picking Boba up and walking to the bedroom. Setting him on the foot of the bed, I crawled under the covers and tried to sleep. The nicotine had me wired, so I tossed and turned for a long time. When I did get to sleep it was not for very long and it was not restful. The following night my sleep was short and restless as well, leaving me exhausted for the start of the workweek.

Monday evening, when I got back to the apartment, tired and cranky from a bad day at work, I found it empty with the lights off. Lena should have been home for two hours at that point. She had not texted or called to tell me she was going out for any reason. Slightly worried, I pulled out my phone and texted her.

Where are you?

I set my phone on the counter and started to cook dinner. When I had finished, Lena still had not returned. Sitting down to eat, I checked my phone before I dug in. No reply. She finally showed up as I was getting ready for bed.

"Where were you?" I asked, confronting her as she walked in the door.

"Out with some work friends."

"Why didn't you let me know?"

"I told you last week that a bunch of us were getting together tonight."

"No you didn't."

"Yes I did. You just forgot, like you always do."

"Well why didn't you respond when I texted asking where

you were?"

"You texted me?"

"Yes."

"I'm sorry, I must not have heard it, it was loud in the bar," she apologized as she pulled her phone out of her purse and checked it. "You did text me."

"Of course I did, did you think I was lying?"

"No, sorry, it's just a figure of speech. Where's Boba?"

"What do you mean 'where's Boba?' I thought you had taken him with you."

"I put him in his kennel when I left this morning, I haven't been back till now. You mean he's not here?"

"No."

"Then where is he?"

"How should I know?"

"Do you think he got outside somehow?"

"How would he manage that?"

"I don't know maybe the maintenance man was in here and accidentally let him out."

"Out of his kennel? By accident? Really?"

"Can we just go look outside please?"

"Fine, let's go," I said and twisted the patio door blinds open. As soon as I did so, Lena screamed. Looking out on the patio, I saw Boba lying there in a bloody heap. He was not moving.

"Call a cab, now," I said and hurried out to the patio. Pressing my ear against Boba's chest, I listened for a heartbeat and breathing, but heard neither. Picking him up, I pinned him tightly to my chest and paced back and forth while we waited for the cab to arrive. When it rolled up, we piled inside.

"Emergency animal hospital and please hurry," I instructed the cab driver.

"You can't bring that thing in here," he replied.

"Please, it's our dog, he's hurt bad. It's an emergency," Lena begged as tears streamed down her cheeks.

"Fine, but you better not get any blood on my seats," he responded gruffly and shifted into drive. Ten minutes later we arrived at the animal hospital and checked Boba in. A vet took him back, then returned a short time later, alone.

"I'm sorry, but he was DOA, there really was nothing we could do."

"What happened to him?" I asked as Lena broke down into sobs beside me.

"Mauled, by another dog most likely. Do any of your neighbours have dogs?"

"We live in an apartment building, like half of us have dogs."

"Any of them particularly aggressive?"

"Not that I know of."

"Something you might want to check into."

"What are you going to do with the remains?"

"Incinerate them, unless you'd prefer to bury them?"

"Incineration, please."

"Will do. I'm truly sorry for your loss."

"Thanks."

Lena continued to weep during the entire ride home. When we arrived back at the apartment it was very late and we both collapsed into bed. The next day Lena called in sick to work, taking what she called a "mental health day." Returning home from my shift, I found her sitting on the couch staring at the TV, but the TV was turned off.

"Hey, anybody home?" I asked jokingly, waving a hand in front of her eyes.

"Home," she whispered in response.

"Hey, you okay?"

"Yes."

"What's up?"

"Nothing. Tired."

"You're being pretty short all of a sudden."

"Sorry."

"It's okay," I said as I slipped my phone out of my pocket to check an incoming text. As I typed a reply, I noticed Lena pull out her phone and begin typing too. When I looked up I saw her watching me out of the corner of her eye and moving her thumbs around her keyboard, seemingly randomly.

"Who are you texting?" I asked.

"Who are you texting?" She asked back.

"I asked you first."

"You first."

"It's nobody, just somebody from work. What about you?"

"Nobody."

"Are you sure you're okay? You seem very out of it."

"Okay."

"You must really be tired, why don't you go to bed?"

"Go to bed."

"Yeah, that's what I said, go to bed."

"Yeah," she said and stood up. Moving jerkily, she disappeared into the bedroom.

"Bet she didn't eat today, she's going to be the death of herself," I muttered and went about making myself some dinner.

I never saw Paul again, but during the first week after our encounter in the park, I had borderline panic attacks every time I sat at the bus stop, afraid that he would show up. Over the weeks following Boba's death, Lena became increasingly distant. Many nights I would come home and find her gone. She would stagger in during the wee hours of the morning, visibly intoxicated, and when I would ask where she had been, she would brush me off with a quick comment about going out with some friends. Eventually I just started to pretend I was asleep when she got home. If she did not care enough about our relationship to communicate with me, then I would give her exactly what she wanted. Either she did not notice or just did not care because she never mentioned it, which frustrated me to no end. Sometimes I felt bad about being so stubborn, but I was done trying to talk, it was her turn.

The silence seemed to drive a wedge between us and Lena

stopped being intimate with me. We no longer lived together; we just inhabited the same apartment. Anxiety and sadness over our deteriorating relationship brought on a bout of insomnia for me, which only compounded our problems, leading to severe paranoia on my part. I became convinced that she was seeing some other guy, but I did not have any real evidence beside the changes in her behaviour. On the rare occasions when she was home, I tried to swipe her phone to check her texts and call log, but I could never find it anywhere. She had to be hiding it from me because she knew I was onto her.

Then on one of the few nights we were both at home, I walked into the bathroom and found all the evidence I needed. There, on the bathroom counter, sat a bottle of contact lens solution. Lena did not even own glasses, let alone wear contacts; she had perfect vision and so did I. Snatching the bottle off the counter, I stormed out of the bathroom and thrust the bottle in Lena's face.

"Who is he?" I demanded.

"What?"

"The guy you're seeing, who is he? Some dude from work?"

"Are you high?"

"Answer the question."

"Don't you dare try and tell me what to do."

"Why aren't you denying it?"

"I shouldn't have to, you should trust me."

"I know you've been up to something and I'll prove it, just you wait."

"You're losing it."

"You just say that because you know I'm on to you."

"Psycho, that's what you are, a psycho."

"Bitch," I hissed and cocked a fist to slug her, but froze when I realized what I was doing. I glanced at my raised fist, then at her. Dropping my hand, I hurriedly grabbed my jacket and keys and flew out the door.

With no idea as to where I was going, I headed down the sidewalk, just putting one foot in front of the other, lost in thought. I could not believe I almost hit her. Maybe I really was losing it. Who was I kidding? I may have been acting a little too jealous lately, but it was her fault I was doing these things. She made me act this way because of the way she was behaving. She really had nobody to blame but herself.

Eventually I came upon a hole in the wall tavern and went inside. It was empty save for the bartender. Sitting down in a dim corner, I ordered a beer. Whenever I finished a beer, I raised a finger to the bartender to call for another. Thus my evening went, drinking silently in the corner, until the bartender shut down early because the place was dead.

Downing what remained of my last beer, I tossed a handful of bills on the table and stumbled back out to the sidewalk. Just down the block I found a liquor store. I went inside and bought a couple tallboys of some cheap beer. Stepping back outside, I pulled a can from my shopping bag and cracked it open, sipping it as I went on my way. Without realizing I was doing it, I walked to Wichita Park.

Drunkenly swaying down the same trail that Paul had attacked me on, I saw something standing off in the shadows that looked out of place. Curious, I crept toward it until I could make out what it was; a tent. Stopping a few feet away, I stood still and listened for the sounds of human habitation, but heard none.

"Yoo-hoo," I called, banging on the side of the tent, "anybody home?"

No response. Unzipping the front flap, I stuck my head inside. Nobody there. I crawled inside and sat down. Taking a long swig, I finished my beer, tossed the can aside, and popped the other one open. Wanting to stretch out, I laid on my back and balanced the can on the centre of my chest. I stared at the can and watched it rise and fall with the rhythm of my breaths, thinking about the first time I met Lena.

It was during college. I had a campus job working weekends as a security guard. One rainy night at the end of exam week I was doing a foot patrol around campus and I heard a woman screaming. Turning a corner into an alley I saw the woman, clad in raincoat and boots, jumping in puddles, laughing and screaming with joy. When she heard my footsteps she looked up at me for a moment, staring at me with the most striking eyes I had ever seen. They were gorgeous. She invited me to join her and we spent all night walking around campus, jumping in puddles and talking. The next day I invited her over to my apartment and we closed ourselves in there together for what felt like weeks. Not too long after that we moved in together. It was her eyes; those beautiful, mischievous eyes.

Waking with a start, I found myself face down on the tent floor. Something had been shaking my body just a second before. A heavy, metallic odour hung in the air and I could feel a presence nearby. Paul. He had found me again. A hand grabbed my shoulder. Rolling over quickly, I flailed at him. The back of my hand caught him solidly on the cheek with a loud smack. Before I had time to process what was happening, he flipped me back over and pinned me to the ground, wrenching my hands behind my back. I felt something clamp tightly around my wrists and then I was dragged out of the tent and yanked to my feet.

"You're under arrest. I'm booking you for assaulting an officer and resisting. Do you understand what I'm saying to you?" An unfamiliar voice, not Paul's, questioned from behind me as I was propelled forward.

"You... who... huh?" I spluttered, casting my head about wildly, confused and still very drunk. Then I saw them. Off in the darkness near the tent glowed a pair of golden eyes, like those of a cat, but larger. Witch's eyes.

"Witch! She's real, we need to run," I screamed and thrashed against the officer's grip, trying to get free so I could run far away.

"Stop resisting," he ordered and slammed me against the car.

"We have to go, she's out there right now. Please."

"Watch your head," the officer said, cautioning me as he put me in the backseat of his squad car.

As we pulled away from the park and sped down the road, I saw a dark figure, on all fours, hurry out to the curb and run alongside the car. The figure turned its head towards me and I saw golden, glowing eyes, and the white gleam of a mouthful of teeth turned up in a wicked grin.

"She's following us. Speed up speed up!" I said.

"Shut up."

The figure kept pace with us for a couple blocks, then loped off into the trees when we reached the edge of the park. The officer took me down to the police station and booked me, throwing me in the drunk tank. I called Lena to bail me out, but her phone went to voicemail, so I left her a message pleading with her to come get me. She showed up a couple hours later and got me out without saying a single word to me. The cab ride home was filled with a tense silence.

"Lena, I'm so sorry for the way I acted earlier," I said when we got inside the apartment.

"I'm going to take my contacts out," she replied, her voice devoid of emotion, and walked into the bathroom, closing the door behind her. Distracted by her coldness, it took me a moment to realize what she had actually said.

"But Lena," I said, pushing the bathroom door open, "you don't wear..."

She turned around and a murderous grin crept slowly across her face. Her eyes blazed, shimmering and golden under the incandescent light.

"No," I exclaimed and took a step back, bumping into the doorframe. A waft of that heavy metallic odour smacked me in the face.

"Oh yes," she said with a giggle and let loose a long, spine-tingling wail, lunging at me. Tackling me to the floor with a wall-shaking crash, she clambered onto my chest and gouged violently at my cheeks with her fingernails, staring me in the eyes the whole time. I let out a scream, but it died in my throat as her eyes entranced me. Losing myself in their glow, I began to lose my senses and became increasingly unaware of what was happening. Letting out a desperate, visceral roar, I snapped out of the trance and gripped her face between my hands. Digging my thumbs into her eye sockets, I sat up and bashed her head into the doorframe. I continued bashing, blood splattering across my face and neck, until her body went limp.

Dropping her head, I scuttled away and looked at her lifeless body lying in the doorway. A bitter wail escaped my lips and sobs overtook me. Leaning against the wall, I stared at her and tapped my head against the wood of the doorframe, continuing to weep. A short time later the police arrived.

HEADLINES

BY STEPHANIE AYERS

Will I ever sleep again?

Everywhere I go, I look over my shoulder. Will they attack? Am I safe?

Will I ever stop fearing again?

They haunt me at night with their knives and guns and angry faces. Every headline I read I know could be me.

"Six dead in murder-suicide."

I shiver. Are we next?

What will be the last straw that makes them crack? Every step I take, every move I make, I never know what will set them off.

How do you move on? How do you relieve the fear?

This is not living, this is surviving. I want to live.

But how? How is that accomplished when they can find me?

This life as I know it has ended, but I don't want another. I just want to be.

Happy. I want my happy back. "Only you can decide your happiness."

Bularkey. I had happy, until they stole it and replaced it with fear.

Fear for me. Fear for my children.

Shadows creeping up on me in my sleep, knife at the ready.

"Six dead in murder-suicide."

Who do they think they are?

This is my home. Mine.

And then they invaded with their nasty talk and disrespectful attitude, their "you're not as smart as me" games, their needling until you react crap.

Fists raised in faces. Bodies towering over smaller bodies. Bruises, chokeholds, and "Fuck you, bitch!" daily.

In my home.

Fear. I hate it.

If I don't feel safe, how can my kids feel safe?

Is it all in my head? Acts to test my sanity?

Fear. I live it.

Nine months of escape wasn't long enough. They came back.

Fear.

And no one understands but me.

No one senses the trembles under my skin, sees the shaking fingers, comforts the elephant tears draining from my eyes.

I'm not a bitch. I'm scared.

I'm deaf and I'm scared. I'll never hear them coming.

"Six dead in murder-suicide."

Will mine be the one you read next?

THE DRIVE

BY R. G. WESTERMAN

The colourful jungle bird stares back at me from the cover of the cereal box. I stand in the grocery store staring straight ahead, with empty shelves stretching, vacant on either side of me. The front window of the building is long since smashed during the riots of the previous weeks.

Three months ago the world as we know it came to an end.

No one knows how it started. Rumours and theories flourished. I have heard everything from government weapons to genetic food modification gone awry. First, there were news reports of a mysterious illness. Headlines and sound-bites blared on every screen about a super-flu spreading throughout the country.

I have now been infected for five days.

I grab the box of cereal and start to walk back to the front of the store. Just down the other end of the deserted aisle, I see my wife's mother, also looking for any food left on the shelves. Her skin has a healthy flush, indicating that she has escaped infection so far. Around her head and neck, she wears a wrapped towel, soaked in vinegar. The healthy people do this sometimes, the theory being that the scent is supposed to mask their presence to those already turned. I want to tell her this towel tactic does not work.

My sense of smell has become more intense since the onset of the infection. Even now, I can reach beyond the powdery talc scent and could make out the dusty aroma of those roaming outside the building; the acrid stench of the dead, and the florid layers of pollen that hang in the air touched by the scent of diesel and death.

I watch my mother-in-law for a moment. Behind her, I see the broken window of the store. Out in the street, some of the others move around slowly, still plodding through the motions of their lives' routines long since left behind them .

We are creatures of habit, even to the end. Those turned could still be seen downtown carrying dusty briefcases, bumping into walls, and walking towards jobs that no longer exist. It is almost comical. Sometimes through the boarded windows of our house, I see people, succumbed to the sickness, plodding down the sidewalk with the ragged remains of a dog leash dragging behind them.

She turns toward me, her hands grasping a few cans of food. I see her eyes settle into a look of recognition and sadness as I approach.

"Hello," I say.

"How are you feeling," she asks, looking at me with lines of concern etched into her forehead.

"It's really not so bad. It's not painful at least."

"And Samantha... Is she...?" The question hangs in the air. My young daughter waits at home secure, safe, and healthy.

"She's fine. Samantha's okay."

Her hand flutters to her throat and she adjusts the fabric out of nervousness and relief.

She leans in and whispers, "They say there are safe houses starting to form. Some people are going into the caves. Also the army base to the west of here. How much time do you have?" As soon as she finishes her face falls, regretting the words.

"It's all right. I have about two days left."

"Maybe you can get her to the army base. One of the safe houses is located there. They have food and medicine I've been told."

"You can take her?" I ask, but her gaze drops to the floor betraying her answer.

"I can't leave," she says as she steps back towards the front of the store, clutching the meagre rations to her chest. "West. Take her west."

I walk into the kitchen from the backdoor. Pausing at the pass-through window, I see my daughter sitting cross-legged on the couch, the glow of the television dancing across her wide-eyed features. She turns when she hears the door.

"Hey, Daddy." She smiles at me.

"Hi, Chipmunk." I smile back.

These past few weeks have been hard on her. I am not certain just how much she knows. I think she understands that I am sick, that her mother is gone, and that the world has changed. But I also know that her child mind holds much more wisdom than I give her credit for. I walk in and sit next to her. She snuggles in under my arm, just like always. We sit for a minute. It hurts me to be that close to her, but I let her. I want her to have some kind of moment to remember. She has lost so much already.

"Listen, sweetie," I say, pausing the cartoon. Her pink-cheeked face turns towards me earnestly. "We are going to go on a trip."

"Where are we going?" she asks.

"We are going to someplace where people aren't sick anymore,"

"And you can get better?" Her eyes widen.

"We'll have to see. But I want you to go and pick out your favourite animal, okay? And I'll get the car ready."

"Okay," she says and scampers off to her room. I go to the closet and pull out her little pink suitcase; I had packed for her after my wife got sick. It includes several changes of clean clothes, extra shoes, and, tucked into the inside pocket, a photo of the three of us at the zoo from the year before, when my Samantha's world still existed.

Half an hour later, we are driving down the highway towards the amber sunset. I watch her through the rearview mirror off and on while I drive. She stares out the window for a while and then holds up her stuffed elephant so it can also look out the window. Before we get to the interstate I stop by my mother-in-law's house. She greets me at the door but does not open the chain lock.

"Come with us," I say when I see her face through the opening.

"No," she says with firm intent. "Please. Just take her and she will be safe." Behind her, I can sense that she is not alone. A strange sound emits from the room behind her, almost like a dog snarling.

"Is everything alright?" I ask. I see fear and panic in her eyes as she darts her head back and forth from me to whoever or whatever lie behind the door.

"Yes, everything is just fine," she says with false cheer.

"Come with us," I plead again. "She's going to need you,"

"And I need to be here!" She spits the words between clenched teeth. "I can't leave. I won't."

Finally, I understand. Her husband had not died. Not in the traditional sense. He is still here with her. I realize then the source of the strange sounds coming from inside.

"Please just go," she whispers.

I turn back to the car without a word.

We drive steadily. The sun slips beneath the horizon ahead and darkness descends. Samantha sleeps in the back seat with her cheek leaning against the seat belt, shadows and moonlight falling over her. The car speeds into the darkened highway, trees rushing by on either side.

I think about my wife, Audra.

And about how I killed her.

Everything had been mostly normal before she fell ill. We both worked at our jobs. Samantha kept attending her second-grade class. The sickness existed in our periphery, nothing more than a passing headline on the evening news.

Then my wife woke up not feeling well. Sluggish and fatigued. Just a bug, she insisted. At that point, they already closed Samantha's school for the week due to a flu epidemic. Audra did look quite pale, but she said she would take a day off to rest. The following morning she looked much worse. Her skin had an alarming cast to it, yellowish, almost white. The dark circles around her eyes marked in stark contrast.

She went to work, waving off her symptoms. By noon, she had returned home. When I saw her at the door, leaning unsteady on the door frame, I rushed to help her. She moved slow, and I lead her straight to the bedroom so she could lie down.

"It must be a forty-eight-hour thing," she said, laughing it off as I tucked the blankets around her.

Already my mind was racing, creating scenarios to keep Audra away from our daughter. No one knew what this sickness was or how it would manifest in the end. Some parts of the country were under quarantine. Travel restrictions had been put in place and in some places, quarantines were being put into effect.

By the third day of Audra's deterioration, her eyes took on a steely focus and I kept finding her standing in odd places just staring off into the distance. That afternoon I could not find her. I searched the house, frantic, only to find her in the backyard gazing at the maple tree. I approached her and she turned to me, a serene smile dancing on her lips.

"Can you hear it?"

"Hear what?" I asked.

"Shh, listen." She raised her palm to quiet me and a soft breeze lifted her hair. "The birds."

A flock of starlings occupied one of the trees across the yard, but I could not hear anything specific to what she mentioned.

"What about them?" I asked gently.

"Not just those. Past that. I can hear the starlings. And then I can hear the hawks in the pine trees."

The evergreen forest bordered the eastern edge of town, but the closest border was at least twenty-five miles away. The wildness in her eyes scared me, and when she spoke I heard an unnatural desperation in her voice. I put my arm around her, and she tucked herself into me. The uneven breathing and lifting of her shoulders betrayed her crying.

"Shh," I said. "What is it?"

"I'm scared," she said as her fingers curled into the fabric of my shirt. "I'm so scared. Something is happening, and I don't know what. I'm losing myself."

I pulled by arms around her, holding her as tight as I could.

"Please," she said. "Just keep her safe. Keep Samantha safe from whatever this is."

"I promise," I said, desperate that the power of my words could extend the same promise to her as well.

As time passes, I become more aware of just how much danger my daughter is in by being around me. The car windows are closed, but the air filtering in through the vent beckons me with the scents from the forest alongside the highway. Birds, squirrels, deer. All with healthy flesh and pulsing blood that would quench my growing hunger.

I hear them. I hear everything out there in the forest. Beyond that, I pinpoint the remaining few people, one young couple holing up in a basement with the furniture piled in front of the door. Three blocks beyond them in the cafeteria of a schoolhouse is a woman alone and afraid, based on the metallic scent of adrenaline that seasons her blood.

My cravings increase with each passing moment.

I think about Audra again and how difficult those last few days must have been for her. Samantha knew her mother was sick, and my little girl had been worried. I tried; I did my best to keep her away. I didn't know what else to do. So little was known or understood about the sickness. Samantha had spent the morning in her room playing on the day my wife died. Audra had gotten up, seemingly better that day, still pale but with a little more energy.

"I think I'd like to go for a walk," she said to me, almost casual.

"Sure," I said. "It might do you some good. Do you want me to come with?"

"No. I think I'd like to go alone."

I looked up at her from my seat at the dining table. Her navy t-shirt offset the tone of her porcelain skin and her uncombed hair framed her face.

I nodded, unsure why I felt an uneasy knot in my chest. She walked out the door, her thin hand resting for a split second on the door frame. Out the window, I watched her approach the corner and turn down the block. This was the last moment that I ever saw her as my Audra.

A half an hour passed and she had not returned.

I told Samantha I was going to find her mother and would be back in a few minutes. Out the door I turned the opposite way that Audra had gone, hoping to meet up with her if she had circled the block. Also concerned that she might have fainted and that I would find her lying in a ditch somewhere in the neighbourhood.

I wish that was how I had found her.

The first house I came to, I heard strange sounds coming from the inside, snarling and screaming. I became aware of the quietness of the streets around me. No cars, or birds, or chattering neighbours, just the unnatural silence compounded by that gurgling, strangled screaming.

A sickening cracking sound broke the screams off, and this

brought me up short. It was then that I noticed the blood on the sidewalk from the next house over, a bright red swath painted down the pavement towards the open door three houses down, as if someone had dragged a wet sponge along the walkway.

I approached slowly.

The door to our neighbours house stood open, hanging on the hinge like a drunken mouth. The sound met my ears and a darkened form crouched in the shadows, leaning over something stretched on the floor. My eyes did not comprehend what I was seeing. For a moment, my vision became a series of shapes pieced together into a nonsensical image. The crouched figure turned towards me.

My wife's face met my gaze, but the eyes did not belong to Audra. Blood framed her mouth and she bared her teeth in a grotesque grin. I backed away, distancing myself from the scene before me. Her eyes trained on me like a predator.

"Daddy?" Samantha's voice cut through me like a knife. She must have followed me. I kept my eyes on the creature that was once my wife.

"Sammy, get back." I did my best to suppress the tremor in my voice. "Go home and lock the door. Right now, Samantha."

From her vantage point on the sidewalk, I knew she couldn't see anything inside the house. I, however, could see that the eyes that were once focused on me now turned on my daughter.

I press my foot down on the gas pedal and we speed further into the night. The hum of the engine does little to distract me from the sound of my daughter's soft breathing.

Morning arrives, small lacy tendrils of light spreading into the sky. I drive faster than I should.

"Daddy, where are we?" Samantha's just waking voice asks me from the back seat.

"We are almost there, Chipmunk."

Up ahead I see the entrance to the military complex. I slow the car and approach the chain link gate, locked and reinforced with barbed wire across the top. I see the tall metal towers with insect-like camera eyes peering down at us. A few miles inside, the reinforced steel bunkers is a group of people, more than fifty, all healthy. I can smell them.

Beyond the fences, in the outlying forest surrounding the chain link fence, I sense the others, the ones like me but lost to all reason. So many of them are hiding in the forest, well into the hundreds. When I stop the car, they sense me and turn their mindless shuffling bodies towards us. They want the girl and, given time, they would get her. We only have a few moments before they arrive.

"Okay, Samantha, this is where it might get a little bit scary, okay?"

She gazes at me with steady eyes, clutching her stuffed elephant to her chest. "Okay,"

"I want you to do exactly as I say. Can you do that?"

"Yes." her tiny voice wavers between confidence and uncertainty.

"First, we have to get out of the car." I can see by her eyes that she understands what danger this poses. "But I'm going to hold on to you, okay? I won't let you go. Do you understand?"

"Yes. I understand."

"Are you ready?"

Without answering, she scrambles up to the front seat and climbs into my lap. Her arms wrap around my neck and her voice whispers into my ear. "I love you, Daddy."

"I love you too, Chipmunk."

Without another word, I open the car door and rush out. She holds onto me with arms and legs keeping her face buried against me. I shout at the nearest camera.

"Hello!" I call with everything I had. "Open the gate! I know someone is there! Open the gate!"

I see shapes coming out of the forest. All they know is that I have meat, fresh, living meat. They want it. I know this because

I feel it too. Samantha is running out of time.

"Sammy, lift up," I say to her.

"No, Daddy, I don't want to see," she whimpers.

"Let the camera see your face," I say. "That's all. Just look up at the camera."

She lifts her head to the camera and a distant frantic sound from deep inside the compound meets my ears.

I turn towards the creatures walking towards us from the woods, grey lifeless shells of humans putting one foot in front of the other. I turn back towards the camera.

"If any of you can hear me. This is my daughter and she is not sick! Someone needs to let her in the gate!"

After a moment a woman crests the hill just inside the metal fence, running. She carries a rifle in both hands and runs towards us. She motions to the camera, waving one hand overhead in a sweeping gesture. The gate begins to swing open, and she levels the gun at me.

"Put her down!" the woman orders. "You have one chance if you can understand me!"

I lower Samantha onto her feet and push her gently towards the slowly opening gate. She begins to cry and cling to my arm. The woman edges towards the opening keeping the gun on me. We both reached the gate at the same time and she places a hand on Samantha's shoulder. My eyes meet those of the woman for a moment. Enough for her to see how sick I am and for me to see the tears gleaming in the corners of her eyes.

"Keep her safe," I whisper.

The woman nods once.

With gentle arms, she guides my daughter away from me and safely behind her. I stand motionless as my daughter cries out for me. As soon as they are clear the woman reaches forward and slams the gate shut with an echoing metallic clash.

I watch them for a few moments, the girl pushing away from the woman, crying and clinging to the fence. The woman stands close to her whispering words to the child. The sound of the others behind me made me only slightly aware that there was food elsewhere. The tide had shifted. A deer had broken its leg and lay injured just inside the tree line. I turn away and join the others marching back into the darkened forest.

GOLD AND SHADOWS

BY LAURA JOHNSON

The day my grandfather died, my shadow spoke to me for the first time.

I was curled up on my bed in the fetal position. A near-empty box of Kleenex teetered on the edge of the nightstand, tissues overflowing the wastebasket and strewn about the floor, like lilies. Everything hurt. My nose was chapped. My throat was raw. My eyes stung. My head throbbed. More than anything, though, my heart ached, and that was a pain no pill or cream could cure.

All the while, I ruminated on my grandfather, trying to preserve my memory of him before his illness.

I'd taken him for granted.

I remembered the beginnings of the disease, before anyone had told me the diagnosis. It was Thanksgiving and the turkey was in the oven, flooding the house with savoury smells while the wind blew a flurry of fiery leaves across the frost-glazed backyard. We were all gathered in the living room, sipping tea and coffee by the fireplace, catching up on the latest family gossip while awaiting dinner. Curled up in the corner of the couch, I tapped my pencil against the clipboard perched on my knee, stuck on a poem I was writing.

"Grandpa," I said, "can you help me think of expressions

with 'golden'?"

My grandfather had been quite the punster, the kind of man who made jokes about cemeteries being so popular, people were "dying" to get in. It was our little game to banter back and forth in a way that made the rest of the family groan. While Kayla had bonded with my grandmother over knitting and crochet, we had bonded over wordsmithing and wordplay. My grandfather was man whose mind wove together words like a spider, and I admired his wit and sharp memory.

After a moment, he said, "How about golden egg, golden goose, or golden age?"

"I have those, but thank you."

"Or fool's gold, heart of gold, good as gold..."

"Oh, I hadn't thought of—"

"Golden egg, golden goose, golden age..."

"Grandpa, you've said those things already."

He only nodded. "Fool's gold, heart of gold, good as gold..."

Abandoning my clipboard, I clasped his knee. "Why don't I tell you how school is going? I'm hoping to go to grad school next year."

He smiled. "I did a Masters in English Literature, too, you know..."

Conversation returned to normal for a whole five minutes, when he started up again: "Golden egg, golden goose, golden age..."

I thought distracting him had broken the cycle. I had no idea what had happened, only that I was suddenly freezing. Looks of unease passed between my relatives. My mother rose. She took me aside and quietly explained that my grandfather was in the early stages of Alzheimer's disease, had been for a while.

"I didn't want you to worry about it," she said.

"What about Kayla?"

Silence hung between us. "We told her not to tell you. We didn't want you to worry."

My whole family, I learned, had known for months and left me in the dark. To them I was made of glass, something to be

93

handled with care, bubble-wrapped in ignorance. And so I had found out about his disease by accident, on a "bad day."

My memories of my grandfather changed after that, shifting from bringing joy and fondness to premature grief and pain. I knew he was going to slip away, starting with memory gaps here and there. Progressing, perhaps, to no longer remembering my name. It would only get worse with time. His golden years were over. In his presence I envisioned Death holding his shoulder with spectral fingers.

George R. Elliot was right; nothing gold can stay.

Now, anything reminding me of my grandfather choked me. His funeral was in two days, but the past few months had been a funeral. I had been grieving for a man still alive; now I grieved a man just passed. At that point I did not want to feel anything. Not sadness. Not dread. Not grief. And especially not guilt for the grief.

It was in the midst of these thoughts that I felt a presence in the room, like how the air becomes humid before a thunderstorm moves in. Pale January sunlight crept through my shutters, casting a wan glow on the walls; where the light failed to reach, the darkness stirred.

A voice interrupted my sobs. "I can take the pain away," it whispered, "if you let me."

Crouched on the end of my bed was a shadowy silhouette, its face featureless except for quicksilver eyes. Diaphanous wings draped from its shoulders. I rubbed my eyes and pinched the soft skin of my elbow, convinced I was dreaming. Instead of disappearing, it lay down next to me and enveloped my body with its wings. Ice seeped into my mind, my skin.

"You don't need to feel a thing," it said. "Sleep, stay with me." Its words were soft endearments, consolations, balms for the ache in my chest. A local anaesthetic. Tears soaked my pillow as I fell back asleep, but in my dreams I could escape the pain.

The air at the funeral was thick, as if a miasma had descended upon the spirits of my family and the other mourners. I don't remember much of it; perhaps it was my general sense of disconnect. My body was present, on auto-pilot through the social niceties, but my mind was elsewhere.

Years ago, I purchased my grandfather a wool scarf in Scotland with his family's tartan on it. I'd bought two, in fact, so we could match but never gave it to him. My grandparents were downsizing to a smaller, more manageable place, and my mother told me he eventually wouldn't remember the significance of it anyway. Now both of them were draped across my dresser next to a photograph of the two of us playing a duet, him on the trumpet, me on the clarinet. I remembered rehearsing for that concert, nervous about playing in front of the church congregation but glad that I had him beside me.

Now, even my happy memories were stained with tears.

Everyone around me was weeping, but my shadow wiped away my tears before they formed. Numbness clung to my insides like frost, but there was no pain; it was as my shadow had promised. For once, I felt nothing save an emptiness that gnawed at my chest, like water hollowing out a glacier.

We grabbed Tim Horton's on the way home, and as the snow fell in fat flakes, I remembered how my grandparents once took my sister and I tobogganing in the park near their house. It was a narrow hill with a forest directly at the bottom, so you had to be careful not to slide into a tree or into the frozen river that snaked through it. After, my grandfather would make hot cocoa on the stove and garnish it with marshmallows and dark chocolate flakes. He couldn't cook worth a dime, but he made the best hot cocoa on the planet.

Had made.

Sorrow clawed at me, but my shadow stirred and suppressed the feelings. "Don't cry. Don't let them know you're falling apart. They'll treat you like glass and encase you in bubble wrap." There'd been cards for crisis counselling at the funeral, and I'd taken one. Its sharp corners had comforted me, and throughout the ceremony I had rubbed them until they were blunt and torn.

When Kayla asked me how I was holding up, I said, "I'm fine." She looked straight at me. Her face was still pink from the funeral, her irises a brilliant green in contrast. I turned away and focused on sipping my hot chocolate, swallowing it and tears both. My mask held, I think, since she didn't probe further; she only squeezed my hand, but I think it was more for her than for me.

After, I cried silently in my room. I reached out for my phone to text one of my friends, and then set it down again, the message unsent. "Nobody wants to see you like this," my shadow said. "They'll say you're being over-emotional, that this will go away. But they don't know you like I do. Now sleep."

My eyelids were heavy from a night of restless, on-and-off sleep. I curled up on my bed and shut off.

I'm still not sure if I slept; I certainly didn't dream.

Months passed. Spring came and bloomed into summer, yet the shadow stayed. With it, the chill of winter lingered in my bones despite the constant sunshine. I passed it off as grief. The rest of my family seemed to be doing fine; if they weren't, their masks were more realistic than mine.

"You deserve to feel this way," the voice said. "Your grandfather was alive."

My shadow spoke to me often, especially before bed, when I'd shut off the lights and was alone with my thoughts and the darkness. When I didn't feel numb, I felt guilty. It was a vampire that drained me of energy, eternally thirsty. I considered telling my family about it, wondered if they'd understand or only see the broken pieces of the glass sculpture they failed to protect.

"They won't believe you," it crooned, reading my thoughts. It was a velvet voice in my ear, though its presence was everywhere. I leaned into it, accepted its dark embrace, and buried myself beneath the blankets again. It was midday. Its presence remained even when I closed my eyes, choking but oddly welcome. "They'll tell you to ignore me. Don't you want me to stay?"

I didn't know. It was too much effort to think anymore.

"Blood magic, darling. Blood magic will solve your problems." The shadow's silver eyes gleamed, its voice almost giddy. I had told a week ago I didn't want to feel numb anymore. Now the shadow was trying to ply me with a razor from the bathroom, had been for days. The antithesis of numbness, it said, was pain.

"Blood magic?" I rubbed my arms, but the goosebumps stayed. "No, no. I don't want any more pain. I don't care what you say. This is dangerous."

"But this is a different type of pain, a wound you can watch bleed and mend. When your heart breaks, nobody sees it bleed... It's all in your head where you can't touch it. But hush, I'm here for you."

It slid from the walls, more corporeal than before. I tried pushing it away, but my hands sank into its body and came away coated in an oily black mist that wouldn't come off. I hadn't noticed my shadow grow, not really, but now it was darker, as though someone had sucked the light out of the space entirely. If sunlight were gossamer, then my shadow was a velvet cloak. Except cloaks were supposed to keep you warm, protect you from the elements; this one protected me from my emotions, but kept me numb.

"Go away," I murmured into my pillow, hurling the razor into the wastebasket and rubbing the unbroken skin on my wrists. It was empty, now, of tissues. Had been for a while. "I don't want you here. You make things worse. This isn't healthy."

"You think you can banish me like an imp?" Its laughter was

a throaty rumble. "I'm sorry, sweetheart – you called me, and I came, and I'm here to stay. Oh, don't look so sad. Put on a smile for the public. There's a good girl."

I forced my lips into a grin, though the effort drained me, and tucked away the deadness I felt inside. I peeled myself out of bed like a tongue from a frozen pole but hesitated at the door to my balcony. The golden sunshine made me shiver, at first. It was true; I felt nothing. But I didn't want to anymore. Where I once saw colour, I now saw grey. I noticed some children outside on my neighbour's lawn, kicking a ball around without a true understanding of death, and I envied their innocent play.

My parents weren't home. They'd gone on vacation for a while, just the two of them, and Kayla was off on exchange in Europe for the summer. I was supposed to be focusing on finding a summer job, but I was tired, and my lackluster energy bled into my applications.

"Join me," my shadow said. It danced along the railing despite the daylight. "If you won't take the razor, then let me take away your pain."

I grabbed the balcony and looked down.

I tried forcing away the thought, but it returned, wrapped around my brain, sinking into my mind. The shadow whispered enticing things, sweet nothings, empty promises. Yet part of me yearned, out of sheer curiosity, to know what it would feel like to throw myself off and let gravity play with my body. The sensation of falling. It was not high enough to kill me, probably. The landing would hurt, certainly. How many bones would I break?

I leaned forward. The wind caressed my face, or perhaps it was the shadow's hand guiding me toward the railing. My fingers grasped hard on the metal, though, holding on with an iron grip. The children continued to play. I lifted one foot, preparing to swing it over the railing. Then I saw two figures stroll down the driveway, calling the kids in for lunch. Their grandparents, maybe, from the whiteness of their hair.

The couple looked up at me and waved.

I took one step back, then the other, retreating into my room. Shuddering, I shut the balcony door. What would my grandfather have thought of that? He, living despite knowing his memory was failing? Me, trying to fight a shadow I could not overcome and letting it consume me. I knew, for grandfather's sake, that I had to try. He would not have wanted me to succumb, even if he could not stop his own mental degradation. There was surely light at the end of this dark tunnel.

Again, the shadow read my thoughts. "Even in light, there are shadows; and when the sun sets, the shadows reign. Tell me, girl, who the stronger power is? Shadows can be banished, yes, but light can be smothered, fire extinguished. Shadows return on their own."

"That doesn't stop people from lighting candles in the night. From trying."

I didn't know when the shadow would leave me, if it ever would. But I had to try. Returning to my bed, I picked up my phone dialled the number on the card I'd taken from the funeral, which had lain abandoned on my nightstand for months. The shadow hissed at me, wailing, but I closed my eyes and pretended not to see it, not to hear it.

I cleared my throat and said into the phone, "I need to talk to someone..."

BLOOD EAGLE

BY SARAH ROBERTSON

"Sam? Did you hear me?"

"Hmm?"

Jess rolled her eyes. "I asked if it helps to keep staring at it."

I smiled and shrugged. "I don't know. Maybe." I tilted my head to one side, closing one eye, then the other, then the first eye again. "If I look at it using just my right eye, and position my head just so, the demon in the painting could be smiling." I switched eyes again. "Maybe."

My cousin snorted. "No, he couldn't. Dork."

I opened both of my eyes. "You're right, he couldn't." I crossed my arms. "Fucking Aunt Katherine."

Jess snorted again.

I flung my arms in the air. Over dramatic? Maybe. But in the moment, it felt appropriate. "I thought you were her favourite niece," I whined. Seriously, Jess deserved the beautiful, Victorian house we now stood in. She was the one there at the end, the one caring for Aunt Katherine. They'd shared a bond I never had with our aunt, and frankly, had never wanted. Aunt Katherine was weird.

"Yeah, well..." Jess shrugged. I knew she agreed, but didn't want to admit it.

She snapped her fingers and started wagging one of them at

me. "You know, come to think of it. I must have been her favourite."

"Oh yeah?"

"Yeah. She left me those creepy occult books without making me sign away my soul. You, though? For you there are strict terms for inheriting this old farmhouse." She formed her fingers into claws and tried to imitate the accent of that damn counting puppet on TV. "She's toying with you from beyond the grave. A person only does that to their least favourite relative." Jess smiled, crooked like how you would picture a diabolical sorcerer smiling while casting an evil spell.

"Uh-huh. Thanks." I sighed, looking at the painting again. "I didn't think I would mind that damn thing so much."

The demon stood on its haunches. His skin pulled over his muscular frame, like hide stretched by a tanner. Almost too tight, the skin craving to touch the bone. Its body structure resembled a mythical faun, only with the hooves of a horse, the horns of a ram, and a triangle hole where a nose should be. The creature stood atop a mountain of broken bodies, each of which displayed gaping backs that exposed torn spines and ribs. In the demon's hands, he held a pair of lungs, presumably ripped from one of the poor souls he stood upon. A viscid string of flesh trailed from the lung to his mouth. Behind him, fire surged and licked at a half-charred forest.

So charming.

I tensed. Something touched my cheek. It felt like someone traced an ice cube down the side of my face. That was odd.

I must have reacted more than I realized. Jess frowned at me.

"Are you changing your mind?" she asked, obviously trying to decipher my behaviour.

"What? No. Although I'm tempted. Letting that picture hang over the fireplace almost makes home ownership not worth it." I smirked. "Almost."

"Aunt Katherine did always speak fondly of that painting. With pride. Like she painted it herself, back in the Dark Ages."

I smirked again. "She was really, really old."

"Very funny." Jess picked up one of Katherine's trinkets, a small chalice with two dragons twisted around the stem. Their red eyes, ruby perhaps, stared into the hemispherical bowl. I watched Jess shift it from hand to hand, carefully caressing it with each finger. "Are you sure you don't want me to stay with you tonight?"

Yes, stay. Please. Don't leave me, screamed the little voice inside my head. "No, I'm fine," I ultimately answered. "I've spent the night here before."

"Yeah, but never by yourself."

I glared at my cousin. "I've survived being here by myself during the day, I can survive it at night. It's just a house."

"So... you aren't afraid of the ghosts?"

I shifted my weight. Why did she ask that? I knew she was joking, and I could give her an equally flippant response. But the silence lingered too long, giving Jess too much time to draw her own conclusions. Her sharp stare stabbed deep before she said, "No. Way."

"Jess..."

"I always knew something else lived in this house."

Again, I had no immediate response and the silence dangled.

Jess squealed. "What's been happening?" she asked, her eyes dancing.

"Nothing. Really." I didn't want to talk about it. If I said it out loud, that made it real. I swallowed involuntarily. Who was I kidding? It was already real. "It's just... there's these flowers."

"Flowers?"

I nodded. "Not the whole flower. Just the heads of white tulips that are," I paused, swallowing again, "half decayed."

"What?"

"I–I thought maybe it was something from a friend or family member for the memorial. A nice gesture that went wrong, you know?"

Jess frowned, but slowly nodded.

"But, when it happened again... twice..."

"What?" Jess's gaze wandered around the room as though the

answer to her question could be found there. "Aunt Katherine, what kind of voodoo were you into?"

A good question.

Jess grabbed my shoulders. "You have to let me stay."

I escaped her grip, resting my own hand on her shoulder. I led her to the side door and opened it. "I love you, Jess, and believe me, I want you to. But I need to stay here alone tonight. It's something I have to do."

Jess nodded. "I can respect that." She wagged her finger at me again. "Just promise you'll call if you need anything."

"I will." I hugged my cousin. "Good night, Jess."

"Good night, Sam." She stepped out the door. "Warning you now, I'm going to call first thing in the morning," she said over her shoulder.

"Of course."

I offered a small wave before gently closing the door and locking the top bolt. I sighed. It's time. I glanced at the painting once more before going upstairs to bed. Wait, what? I frowned and looked again. Something was off. Great. A rampant imagination is the last thing I need right before trying to sleep. I walked towards the painting to put my mind at ease. I squinted, studying the stupid beast. I remembered the one claw-hand holding half-eaten lungs. The other arm, though. Had it always been bent like that? I didn't remember him flexing.

"I'm losing it," I said out loud, shaking my head. If he was flexing now, of course he had always been like that. I looked to the demon. "Good night to you, too."

I pulled the covers up to my chin.

"Close your eyes."

I blinked.

"Good start. Try again."

I blinked again, my lids lingering closed a little longer.

I yelped when a mechanical pop from outside rattled the whole house. My body stiffened, adrenaline forcing me to sit up.

My shoulders slumped, though my heart still raced, when I realized where the pop came from. The outdoor generator. I knew it would kick on in the middle of the night. It did it when I stayed here as a kid, too. Scared me back then just as much as it did just now. Proof that, sometimes, knowledge offered little comfort. I instinctively placed a hand on my chest as though it would slow my frantic heart.

"This is ridiculous." Maybe some warm milk would help settle my mind. Or a shot of whiskey.

Whiskey. Definitely whiskey.

I flung the covers to one side of the bed, liberating my legs enough to slide off the other side. My bare feet stuck to the floor. I winced at the uncomfortable peeling sensation that accompanied every step to the stairs. The sound reminded me of the one time I had my legs waxed, only the aesthetician pulled too slowly. I shuddered. Goosebumps tickled my legs.

At the stairs, I clutched the railing. The darkness made it difficult to not fumble my footing while I descended to the bottom floor. Every step sounded like someone ripping off a Band-Aid. Finally, I stepped from the last stair only to have my hand hit a moist spot on the railing.

"Ugh, what is this?" Something dripped through my fingers, but I couldn't tell what it was. My eyes were adjusted to the dark, but the opaque, pudding-like slime was too ambiguous.

Light. I slapped the wall across from the railing with my clean hand. I slid my hand across the wall, my fingertips tapping the textured paper. The light switch had to be near.

"C'mon, you bastard."

While I searched for the switch, a smell tickled my nose. Sweet and floral, but left a lingering metallic coolness in my sinuses. Perfume, surely. I wrinkled my nose. Bad perfume at that. I didn't remember noticing it when Jess was here earlier, but it had to be from her.

Finally, that push-button switch. I traced it with my

fingertips like a blind person trying to read braille; the bumps revealing all I needed to know as long as I could decipher them. Groping the switches and the decorative plate covering them, I found the top button to be slightly higher than the bottom. I pushed it, plunging the button into the wall.

I squinted. For the briefest moment, my eyes were struck by the brightness.

Two light bulbs popped, like gunshots. I yelped, immediately chiding myself for being so jumpy.

One bulb remained. It revealed enough.

I scanned the room. I felt unsure of how to interpret what I saw, skeptical that this was reality and not a dream. The decapitated heads of white tulips littered the room. Not fragile and decaying this time, but fresh and beautiful.

"Who's here!?" I yelled. I clenched my fists. My fingernails dug into my palms, and I remembered... something slimy still covered my hand.

The world slowed. I rotated my gaze to my soiled hand. My fingers trembled.

Blood.

Dark. Viscous. Thick. Blood.

A drop trickled from my hand. I opened my hand a little wider. Through the slits between my fingers, my stare followed the drop as it fell to the ground.

I swallowed. On the floor... Was that... Was that a lung?

The air around my head felt thin. Somehow, I managed to draw in a breath. It rushed back out as a shrill, tumultuous scream. Instinct devoured rational thought. And I ran.

Door.

Where was the door?

Where was the fucking door?

Kitchen.

Run, damn it! Run!

The faster I ran, the slower I seemed to move. In dreams, movement often feels like wading through quicksand. Was this a dream? Maybe it was.

Blood soaked my feet, making my steps unreliable and clumsy. I reached out, half falling, half throwing myself against the door, and whimpered.

Open. The door rattled as I pulled with all my strength. It didn't budge.

I pulled again. Rattle. Again. Rattle. I tried to tear the door from the hinge. I clawed at the painted wood. Anything to escape.

Nothing.

I could hear the stupid generator puttering near the barn. Amongst all the gore and adrenaline, hearing that hum... it connected me to the outside.

Wait. No.

The sound was too low of a resonance to be the generator. I held my breath, straining to hear. The sound was more of a groan or a growl.

And it wasn't coming from outside.

Strands of hair ambushed my face when a blast of warm air assaulted the back of my neck. I shivered despite its heat.

Something spoke.

"Breeeeeeeeeaaaaaaathe."

I started crying. Guttural, visceral, terrible was the voice.

"BREEEEEEEAAAAAATHE."

I whimpered for a moment before swallowing. My throat was dry. But I did as I was told. In through the nose, out through the mouth. Again. And again.

In my peripheral vision, I saw something resembling a hand. Muscular, part claw. It came close to my face, and I closed my eyes. I shuddered when a sharp talon pricked my cheek. The touch was surprisingly gentle.

"I love you," the voice whispered. Now, a soft, strong voice. A voice meant to swoon. Was it the same voice?

I turned around. Nothing. No one. My eyes darted, covering the room. I couldn't stop panting.

The tulips were gone. The lung, the blood, all gone. Every light once burned out now burned bright. My hand was clean.

The generator rudely puttered through the quiet, peaceful night. All was calm, the way it should be. Except for one thing.

The painting. The bodies remained broken, the forest still burned. But the demon. The demon had disappeared.

"What the FUCK is going on?"

Cursed. Cursed. Cursed.

For six-hundred years, the word had echoed in my mind. Like water dripping rhythmically on a rock, slowly eroding and decaying the moss and stone.

Cursed. Cursed. Cursed.

My jaw clenched. A storm churned in my gut, power swelled in my spirit, a wave of warmth. Breath was returning to my lungs. I smiled.

No. More.

I never believed I would be strong enough to overcome the treacherous, old witch who trapped me in this painting. But as time had been callous to her, it had been generous to me. While Katerina and her curse aged, I grew stronger. Admittedly, a pittance of power, though enough to kill the old hag. My destiny of bringing destruction and chaos to the mortal plane was once again in sight.

One person stood in my way. A girl with the name of a boy. All I needed to do was convince her to release me.

She looked at me now. Oh, how I wished she knew I was meeting her stare. She tilted her head. Her long hair fell over her shoulders, spilling downward, and caressing her breast. I envied her hair.

"Fucking Aunt Katherine," said my fair-headed warden.

I couldn't have agreed more.

The homely one behind her snorted. I never liked her. She radiated the same type of magic Katerina possessed. Given the opportunity, she could see to it I stayed imprisoned forever.

I wondered why Katerina had not made her my new warden. Foolish bitch. Although, eventually I would have destroyed the homely one, too. Stolen the breath from her lungs in the same way I stole it from Katerina's. Yes, it seemed Katerina put more thought into her actions than I originally gave her credit for. Eh, no matter. She was still a bitch.

But this other one. Sam. Perhaps I had the strength to... Yes, I could caress her cheek. Her skin, softer than any breath a full-lipped, porcelain-faced virgin had ever presented to me. It made me wish I had a heart. I wanted to feel more for this woman.

She frowned when I touched her. A pang originating in my chest echoed through my body. She ignited a fire in my immortal spirit. One that devouring a thousand lungs, stealing the air from a thousand sacrifices, could never fuel. Perhaps, I didn't need a heart after all.

"Do you want me to stay with you?" I heard the homely one ask.

No, let this night be just for us.

"No, I'm fine," said my maiden. "It's just a house."

She wanted to be alone with me. Me, of all demons. Finally, a night I could show her my love. I would see my fair-headed warden wooed, and she would release me.

But, there was no way around it. It would lead to her destruction.

"Nothing. Really. It's just... there's these flowers," I overheard my maiden say.

I returned my attention to the pair. She'd noticed the gifts I left her.

"Flowers?" asked the homely one.

My maiden nodded. "Not the whole flower. Just the heads of white tulips that are... half decayed."

What do you want from me? My powers are meant to destroy. I can only sustain living things for so long. Perhaps tonight, you will see them for their moment of life.

I sighed to myself. Live flowers. Mortal women want live flowers.

The homely one left. My maiden returned to me. Alone at last. I tried to show her my strength, that I could be worthy of her.

She looked a bit closer. Yes, study my body. This is only a taste of what you will receive, what I can offer.

She shook her head. "I'm losing it," she said. "Good night to you, too."

She... spoke to me. Her voice sounded so much sweeter than any pleas for mercy uttered by those about to be sacrificed. Their offerings of idiotic mortal trinkets — gold, land, virginity — held no interest to me. No, instead, I would perform the blood eagle. I would expose their spinal columns, sever and pull apart their ribs to ultimately wrench free their lungs. The flavour of their breath — fresh and bloody — that alone held my interest. And yet it was her words and not her breath that fulfilled me now. Oh, how I wished I could respond.

Was I truly willing to give up the destruction of the world for the love of a mortal woman? To risk falling back into hell, and wait another 600 years amongst tortured souls to find strength for destruction?

I did not wish to entertain such questions, afraid of the answers. Besides, much needed to be done to prepare for our night alone. I would shower her with gifts, share with her the breath sacrifices of the blood eagles. She would be persuaded by my power and wooed by my strength.

Time was a funny thing. I learned in my years snared inside the cursed painting that mortals regard it with more pomp than an immortal god of destruction. Though tonight I was grateful for the time. I used every ounce of strength I consumed from Katerina's lungs to make this perfect.

The flowers were alive, the lungs were full, and I summoned enough magic to once again walk among mortals. A feat only love could conquer.

Surely my maiden would appreciate such gifts.

I heard her come down the stairs. She turned on the lights. Too bright. We needed it dimmer to set the mood. I extinguished two of the light emitters.

She ran for the side door. No, where was she going? This was a night we were going to stay in.

She clawed at the door, ripping at it as a lioness taking down prey. I could think of only one way to calm her wild spirit. I walked towards her, and gifted her with my breath. She began crying. Yes, it was a truly beautiful night. Dare I ask of her...

"Breeeeeeeeeaaaaaaathe."

Her soft wails touched me. My immortal soul wanted to burst. I asked again.

"BREEEEEEEAAAAAATHE."

She paused. Oh, how she toyed with me.

But finally, she relinquished.

Her breath tasted like honey. Though, truly, it was unlike anything ever given to me before. If I took it, it could sustain me. I could find my full strength.

The Great Fire would burn. Destruction would reign. My purpose would be fulfilled.

I stared at her. Her beauty captivated me, if only I could touch her... I reached out my hand. I stroked her cheek. Flesh on flesh.

No, I could not see her harmed.

"I love you," I whispered in a soft voice I never knew I possessed.

And headlong, into the abyss, I fell.

For her.

MONSTRUM

BY TYLER OMICHINSKI

The quick retorts of gunfire echoed through the night air, the first signs of the chaos that erupted in the compound.

"I told you to double check the schedule," a man in tactical gear, his face covered with a mask and goggles, yelled at his companion over the echoing noise.

"I did double check the schedule, Sal. They've just gone off it." the other man said as he ducked down behind a toppled table for the modicum of cover it provided. Secured, he added to the din, "Reloading."

Sal rose quickly, laying suppressing fire down the hallway towards the remaining guards, before ducking behind a heavy pillar that had once supported a vase that had looked expensive. The second man had knocked it over, smashing it to the ground when he had dispatched the first guard, the one that now lay on the ground.

"At least try to be professional Harv, no real names," Sal said as Harvey rose,

"Well, they didn't know that was my real name until you said something."

"Not like we're going to be killing them anyway."

"You don't need to be so pissy."

"Grenade!" They had both missed the guard pulling one out

of his tactical gear, both had missed whether he had cooked it or not.

"Got it," Harvey stood and kicked the grenade back the way it had come, skittering along the floor.

"Oh sh—" One of the guards managed to get out before the explosion tore him, and the rest who were encamped at that end of the hallway, apart.

Harvey giggled a little, as he shook his head. The ringing in his ears wouldn't clear.

"What were you thinking? You had no idea how much time you had."

"What?"

"You could have died!"

"What?"

"Never mind. Clear your head." Sal shook his head and gestured for the other man to get into cover. He stood, holding his rifle at the ready. He moved up the hallway, ducking into cover as he went. Behind a small table that had been mostly torn apart by the gunfight, between two chairs that would only provide him cover from being spotted immediately, and finally to the circle of the dead and the dying.

He checked each of them, making sure that none would be participating in any gunfights for the rest of the evening. Beyond that, he didn't particularly care. Of the three men who had been there, one was still alive, albeit very bloody.

"Wh—wh—" the man gurgled, trying to form words around the tears in his face and lungs.

"Why?" Sal glanced at the man, before checking to see if any more were coming. "You want to know why?'

The man nodded.

"Use your words."

"Yes." The words were strained, pulled taut with pain.

"Don't worry about it." Sal shot the man once, in the head.

"Why'd you do that?" Harvey said, coming up from behind him.

"They already know we're here."

112

"Not what I meant."

Sal shrugged.

"Softie."

Sal shrugged again. Then he said, "Let's move."

Harvey raised his gun in response, prepared to continue on their slaughter.

Sal moved first, rounding the corner, expecting there to be more guards charging them. There should have been.

"Where is everyone?"

"Why don't I ask them?"

Sal's shoulders climbed a half inch, tension pulling into his back and neck.

"Hey, stay frosty. No use getting worked up."

"This isn't business."

"You don't have to remind me."

The two men leapfrogged over and past each other, moving up the hallway covering each other as they went. They ducked behind modern art sculptures made of red and white arcs twining about, dodged into alcoves that were arranged with chaise lounges, and leaned around corners that weren't the traditional right angles.

"We should be killing this guy just for his decor," Harvey said.

"I kind of liked that sculpture. Before you knocked it over."

"You would. I don't want there to be anything left for anyone."

"Think of the artist though. He worked hard on that."

"On that? Really?"

"You'd be surprised."

It was Harvey's turn to shrug, "No accounting for taste I guess."

He was leaning up against a wall at a frustrating seventy degree angle, trying to figure out a way for the two men to most effectively round the corner when they took the shop. Shots riddled through the wall. Most missed him, but three tore into the meat of his shoulder. His hand tensed then went limp as the simpler parts of his nervous system warred with training and experience. Sal dove to the side and around the corner, surprising the team of four who were moving up on them. He fired, the bullets creating what might as well have been a wall of lead as every round was hurled out of the gun. The ambush turned into a bloodbath, and the latest round of guards collapsed.

Without standing, Sal reloaded his gun and prepared for more. "You okay Harv?"

The man grunted, "We clear?"

"Think so."

"I'm hit. Bad. Gonna try to bind it."

"You're covered."

Harvey slumped to the floor, then lowered his gun carefully next to him. He pulled at the sleeve of his jacked, trying to suss out how bad the damage was. After a few moments, he gave up, and pulled bandages from the supplies he had brought in with him. With one arm, he clumsily wrapped up the shoulder, ensuring that at least the bleeding should slow. That addressed, he reached into another pocket within his gear and fished out a needle.

"Don't take too much," Sal said.

"Just cover me." Harvey said, before he plunged the needle into his leg, depressing the contents into his blood. "Shit that feels good."

Down the hallway Sal was watching, a young man popped his head out. Without bothering to check if he was another of the guards Sal shot this latest person. "Want to just burn this place down?" Sal said, "It would be easier."

"He might survive though. Besides, I want to see his face."

They continued through the building, working their way toward the centre. Their preparation had including poring over blueprints to try to find a way through the building. It was a labyrinth already, and the owner had apparently been keen to continue to add his own flair to it with renovations and alterations.

"Screw this, let's just start cutting through walls," Harvey said when they reached the third dead end.

"It will take too long. He's got to be in the panic room now, exactly where we want him. Stick to the plan."

"You're right."

"As always."

"Are we close?"

Sal didn't answer him, instead turning to backtrack and try another path. "I think it is left here," he said when he stood in front of a gold plated statue of a young woman with tentacles instead of arms.

"Yeah? You remember because of the statute?"

"Don't be gross."

"I'm just saying, you're the one who liked his art before."

"No, I liked one piece of art. This is just..."

"For sickos."

"I didn't say it."

"Didn't disagree either."

"Shut up and come on."

The two men had left piles of bodies behind them, guards that had come up against them. They were tired, but continued to push forward. There were pools of blood behind them, and their footprints crisscrossed the estate, tracking across fur carpets and priceless artifacts alike.

The entire compound was structured, in broad strokes, like a target. There was an exterior building that created a green space within it. Within that there was another building, the inter sanctum of the warlord who had built an empire on blood.

"Just paying him back," Sal had said when they first talked about this plan.

They crossed into and out of the green space numerous times – it was divided by walls that broke it up into numerous smaller gardens and areas. One had a tiger in it, an animal they had almost shot before they realized that it was confined to a cage.

"We'll let you go on the way out," Harvey had promised.

As they continued to move through the complex, they were running out of time. With the rising of the sun, they would no longer have the cover of darkness, and someone would notice that there were no communications coming in or out. By the time they had finally found the entrance to the inner sanctum, the sky was starting to grow lighter.

"We're running out of time."

"There's just two stories. We'll make it."

The building in the centre of the complex was white to survive the heat of the summer, and was a two story building that was the shape of a hexagon. The roof was an only slightly steep set of red clay shingles that would have looked more at home on the Mediterranean. Neither man knew what would be on the inside, so they positioned themselves on either sides of the door before kicking it open.

The inside was a humble abode, arranged more like a large cottage than anything. There was a quaint kitchen and dining area off to one side, with a large fireplace in the centre. It was sunken below the average height of the floor throughout, with seats carved directly into the floor. There were pillows covered in thick fabrics of many colours scattered throughout, and their target sitting there near a fire burning low, waiting for them.

"Three o'clock. Could be people hiding behind the bookshelves," Sal said, low to try to prevent their target from hearing them.

"Gentlemen, please, come in. There's no one else left."

Harvey went first, his gun at the ready.

"Please, come sit. You've already killed everyone else."

"Why aren't you hiding?"

"I've lived this long by knowing how to read a situation. You want me dead, and hiding n a panic room is just going to slow you down, not stop you. If I sit and talk, maybe you're willing to reconsider. I can pay."

"Harv," Sal said.

"Are we clear?"

"Looks like."

"Cover me."

Harvey stepped down into the pit around the fireplace, feeling the warmth from the dying fire.

"So glad you decided to talk," the target said.

"Every man deserves a chance to explain themselves, to talk, don't you think so?"

"A man after my own heart. Now why don't you take your goggles and the mask off," he said with a gesture, "Let me see who I'm talking to."

"No. You treat me without knowing who I am. I like what I hear, you'll see what I look like."

"Ah, an idealist. Very well. What seems to be the problem?"

"You are. We don't like your recent policy decisions."

"Disgruntled constituents. Of course. Anything in particular?"

"You've been making changes lately, ones regarding homosexuals."

The man's face fell, the smile that had been planted across it since they had arrived fled into nothingness. "I understand. I am doing everything I can, but the Western—"

"The Westerners?"

"Yes. So much of what we do relies upon them, we need their money to be able to keep the unsavoury elements at bay."

"So, everything you've done, has been a compromise?"

"Exactly. Trust me, if I could have done more—" Harvey shot him in the knee. The man began screaming.

"Thought you'd never get to it," Sal said.

Harvey shot him again, this time in the other knee. Then a third time in the gut. The man flailed in the pit at the centre of the room, shrieking. It reverberated and echoed throughout the room, sounding like the sweetest music to Harvey.

Sal and Harvey waited until the man grew hoarse from the screams, began to quiet down. When he had his wits more fully about himself, he said "Why–?"

Harvey pulled the mask and goggles off of his face, revealing burns up the entire left side of it. "You made me a monster, so I did something monstrous." They both saw the look of revelation spread across the man's face, remembering the attempted purges from years before, everything he had done in the name of 'ridding the nation of filth'.

Just at the moment of revelation, Sal shot the man in the head.

"It's done now," he said.

"I love you," Harvey said, looking at the other man.

"I love you too. You're beautiful." Harv winced, thinking about the burns on his face. Sal pulled off his own mask and goggles, and pulled the other man close for a quick peck on the lips. "Come on," he said, "we have to let that tiger go yet."

HONOR OF SONS

BY PAUL R. DAVIS

Incense burned on the small shrine. The short, wooden structure had a little roof to keep the most severe elements from defacing the mantras inscribed on the back panel. Scorch marks dotted the small altar as prayers and goods were lifted up to the gods and ancestors.

Sing knelt before the shrine. "To those before me, bless our family so we may have a son to carry on our family line. Without one, our family and your comfort in the afterlife come to an end. To those above me, see fit to give me a son. He will pray to you alongside me day and night for your generosity. We will proclaim the Dynasty good and mandated by the Heavens. To those I don't know, bless me with a son so he might work my fields and give me grandchildren. For this deed, I will give you an altar of your own.

"To all three I pray, and to all three I will give gifts. Please, give this old and righteous man a son. My wife is too old, her body too frail, but find a way." Sing wept, his head in his hands by the end of his pleading. The words became spittle and snot dribbling down his aged face.

The man was old, nearly too tired to work his fields, yet he had no one to work in his stead. His three daughters would be married off to other families, and he would soon have no children in the eyes of his ancestors.

Likely one of his daughters would marry the youngest son of another family, and the son would be offered to Sing in order to work the fields and take on the family name. But he did not want a pity son. Such a gift, due to pride, was to be turned down eight times, and then accepted the on the ninth offering, but Sing wouldn't even accept it then, though it would be a grave insult to the offering family. He sighed, thinking, what was his pride when he would die a broken man over a plow and ox? In old age, he should be able to laze in his bed or sit on the porch while watching his sons work the fields.

The incense burned out, leaving another mark on the shrine. With a grunt, Sing stood, his knees aching. A firm hand grabbed his shoulder, and when Sing turned he saw his friend Fen. Fen was still a fairly young man, his strapping physique netting him a bride quickly. He had one son, the middle one, and four daughters. The first daughter had already been married off and the second was betrothed. His son was starting to grow hair on his face, and that was a sign he could work the fields for the full day.

Fen flashed a smile, "The earth is taking you. Each time I see you kneeling here, I wonder if you'll get up. Good thing I was here to help."

Sing chuckled. "You just want to claim my land."

"Only as soon as my son marries your eldest. Then I'll likely leave you in the dirt." Both men laughed.

Sing said, "Fen, I believe I would gladly give you my daughter. Jao has raised Ling well. If you wish to have your son marry my daughter, I would see it as an honour."

"You would be truly honoured with a son," Fen said, the mirth leaving his face.

Sing looked down. There would be no more children from his wife, Jao. She nearly died giving birth the last time. "This is true, but you only have one. I wouldn't ask."

"Of your own, friend." Fen held Sing's arm. "There are rumours of a woman who gives only sons. She lets any man plow in her fields. At night, you plant your seed, and by the morning the harvest is ready. I want to help you find her, so you can have a son."

The gods and ancestors gave an opportunity for a son, at the price of fidelity to Jao. Sing felt there was a test, but he couldn't figure out which was the right answer.

"Farmers have an abundance of time in the fields to make up stories. I'm too old for fanciful stories, Fen. Only the gods could decide to birth us sons in the time it takes for the sun to set and rise, and they've never visited our village." He sighed, thinking of his prayers. "And they likely never will."

"If you wish, my old friend. I'm only trying to help you fulfill those prayers of yours, since your wife can't." Fen walked away and Sing's chest clenched. He gripped his shoulder and blamed old age before heading home, every step more clouded by the thought of a woman able to give him a son.

When Sing returned home, his eldest daughters, Ling and Min, ran through the small house and jumped into their father's arms. Energetic youth struck Sing's elderly frame, causing bones to complain. He laughed off the aches. In the back of the common room, Jao, his wife, held their one year old daughter, Diao.

Jao smiled at her husband out of duty, the sad smile that killed Sing inside. It was the same smile ever since Diao nearly killed her and Sing refused to risk Jao's life for a boy. Sing thought of the woman Fen told him about, then looked away from his wife. He could still have that son.

Ling and Min shouted how they helped keep the house clean, and that they learned to make dumplings. The girls also churned soil for medicinal roots, which explained the dirty hands.

Jao finally spoke softly. "Girls, your father has had a long day. Give him peace."

Both girls sighed, but only Ling spoke, "Mother, we haven't told him everything yet. Please let us talk to father." Her full brown eyes begged both parents. With how beautiful his daughters were, he could only imagine how hansom his son would have been.

Sing broke the silence as he always did. "Ling, you and your sister can tell me about your day at dinner. My ears hardly work on an empty stomach." He rubbed his belly and gave a crooked smile. The girls laughed. "Show me what you learned to cook."

Jao sighed and shook her head, frowning. Sing knew the look. He knew she would talk to him later about being too close to his daughters. She would remind him they were being raised for someone else.

Dinner continued with the girls telling Sing endless stories of the day, many exaggerated or entirely fictitious. After the girls cleaned up, Sing's daughters asked for a story. Sing consented. He tucked the girls into bed and created a story about magical animals, continuing to weave the tale until the girls drifted off to sleep. Diao was already asleep in her crib, and Jao waited in the bedroom.

When Sing made his way to bed, his wife was naked. A candle dimly lit her body. Sing smiled, though she was aging and had never been a beauty to gaze upon. It was still his wife and there had never been a more subservient and loyal woman.

Sing undressed to prepare for bed. "You raised the girls well. They will make great wives, just as you make a great wife." He moved into the bed and put the covers over him, hiding his body from his wife.

"I raise them for another family. They will marry and we will have no children." She laid on her back and said, "Lay with me, and I will give you a son."

Sing shook his head, "I love you, Jao. Diao almost killed you. Another certainly would. If the child doesn't survive, or if we have another girl, I would live alone. I can't lose you. Even if I were promised a son for your life, I would not trade you."

Jao cried suddenly, turning from Sing. "I shamed you, my husband. I failed to give you a son."

Sing embraced his wife. He kissed her forehead. "Don't be ashamed. You have given me a beautiful family." As Sing blew out the candle, holding his sagging wife, he thought of the woman who bore only sons. She could be the answer to Sing's shame. She could be fruitful in ways Jao had proven incapable. The family could be whole, at the cost of a lesser shame.

The following day, Sing went to the stream for water when he saw Fen sitting at the water's edge. Sing shouted, "You won't grow much like that."

Fen laughed. "I'm wondering what I want to grow. Our wives give us mostly daughters. I'd rather sons. Why isn't the seed taking right, Sing?"

Sing shrugged and dipped his bucket in the water. He eyed Fen and thought how lazy youth could be.

"I can tell you why: bad soil. Dian and Shu went to see the woman the other night. Couldn't stop praising her beauty and fertility. What's a crop of rice to a crop of sons?"

Sing grunted. "You think too highly of those two. They're drunkards and layabouts. Their only child came out crippled because of their drinking. No good, those two. They fill your head with demon tales. Tell me you're better than that, Fen."

"I might go to her. They told me where to find her. Come with me, Sing. You need her more than any of us."

"And what would I tell my wife? For that matter, what would you tell yours?" Sing felt a little guilty. The thoughts occurred, that he would go lay with this woman, but having it pushed so eagerly by Fen made him push back.

"Do you tell your ox and plow how you're going to plant your fields? Your woman is your property. You don't need to tell her what you're doing. You need that son to plant your fields. You need him to one day burn incense at your altar so you can have a blessed afterlife. Having a son will wipe away your shame and hers." Fen went toward his fields. "Time to work. If you want, come with me to see the woman promising sons."

Sing was left alone with his thoughts. With sons, he thought, especially so many so quickly, he would be able to hand over the farm in a little over a decade. The mother would be another woman, but many men took multiple wives. Some only claimed women for a few years, enough to take her blossom and have children while she was at her strongest. The coupling with this strange woman would be for a few weeks at most. If the stories were true, no more than one night. After he ensured his name's future, he would go back to Jao, the dutiful wife. The docile, placid, ever obedient wife.

He wept, heart aching.

The thoughts continued, and it wasn't long until the sun touched the horizon. When Sing returned home, the children were still playing outside. Ling and Min both shouted to their father, but continued to run around in the fields. Warmth filled his chest as he watched them. His daughters were good, strong, beautiful girls, and for a moment he truly thought he wouldn't trade them for all the treasure in the world. Then he pondered if he would trade them for boys. Or would he trade the shame of bedding another woman for a chance to have sons, especially laying with a woman who was with so many men already. The warmth escaped, and he went inside before the girls could see the pained crease on his brow.

When Sing entered the house, his thoughts were drowned by Jao's tears. His wife sat on the floor, weeping, her hands bleeding from indents left by her nails. Sing went to her side and held her. "Jao, what's wrong?"

"Sai, she's gone." Jao buried her head into Sing's chest, sobbing. Her hands wrapped around his arms, the fingers digging into him painfully as her body shook. Her voice was barely above a whisper.

Sing kissed the top of his wife's head, enduring the pressure. "What happened?"

"They found her in the fields. Her husband's gone. Sing...." Jao looked up to her husband, dark eyes welled up with tears. "Her neck was cut. Her blood, it was..." Jao moved back to her husband's chest.

"We will honor her when the sun is high tomorrow and pray the ancestors accept her on our behalf." He kissed the top of her head. "Then I will find Guan's body. Is her body covered?"

Jao nodded and said, "Thank you." The two held each other as Jao wept.

The following day, Sing looked over the local fields hoping to find Guan. Fen said he saw Guan go east a day or so ago, towards the woman. Fen and the rest of the men seemed unconcerned for the most part with the death of Sai. A few of the women had red eyes, but they held their tongues. The village felt gray and barren.

"You should come see her tonight," Fen said.

Sing narrowed his eyes, stopping for a brief moment. "Sai is dead. Guan is missing. Do you have no concern for those around you? Is this woman's womb the only thought on your mind?"

"What is a woman? Guan is off sleeping with the Butterfly. That's what they call her, and how can you doubt such a beautiful name? You worry for Sai? Sai was nothing. We can all see that, Sing. You don't mourn the broken pot. Replace it. Move on." Sing wondered if that darkness was always inside Fen and this simply pulled it out. He prayed to Fen's ancestors that it was something brought out by this Butterfly.

"I'm leaving. I must get Sai to give her a proper ritual at noon. Maybe the ancestors will capture her soul and save her if we do. Slitting throats," he muttered, "this is a monstrous thing."

Fen nearly spoke, but Sing departed swiftly for fear he'd throttle his heartless friend.

When Sing approached the home of Guan and Sai, he found Guan. However, the husband was neither dead nor distressed, but whistling as he worked the land, singing songs of praise to the ancestors and the gods of the earth. He sung about the lightness of loved labor and the joy of lost burdens.

"Brother-in-law," Sing called as he approached, "why do you sing when your wife's soul was released through her throat and she might be denied her place beside your ancestors? I seem to be mourning her loss more than the man who wed her."

Guan's smile grew when he caught sight of Sing. "Why don't you join me in song? You could be the harmony."

"Sai is dead. Your wife is gone. Where is your daughter?"

"I will have sons, and that is why I sing. I laid with the Butterfly, and I will not wait to see if I have sons with your wife's sister. Your wife has proven incapable enough, and I won't risk it's in the blood to have only daughters.

"Sing, you've married the eldest daughter, and no doubt she has been fully harvested, or close to it. Join me with this woman. She will give you sons, too. I will be going to stay with her soon, but for now I make sure there is food for the winter."

A chill settled into Sing's bones. "I should leave. May the ancestors be kind to you, Guan, and return your wits."

"I have my wits. I will have many sons. I will need no woman but my queen. She will give us all sons, and she will give them sons, and continue so one woman can keep our names going."

Sing was out of words for the fool, and walked away. Guan continued his songs of praise to the ancestors and gods while he worked the fields.

Shortly after leaving Guan, Sing met with Fen. Fen said, "The farmers, Dian and Shu went to the woman again. Dian was saying he was bringing his daughters and wife to her tonight. We should go, Sing."

This woman held the answers to Sai's death and why Guan was so happy about it. It would give Jao the peace she was looking for. Sing wouldn't take the offer for sons, he continued to reason. It was for the good of his wife, so she knew what happened to her sister.

"I will go with you to see the Butterfly." The words hurt less than Sing expected.

◆ ◆ ◆

The house was quiet that evening. Jao didn't look Sing in the eyes, and Ling and Min were silent. Even Diao did not cry out. When dinner was finished, Sing packed a pipe and went outside to smoke it. Jao and the children didn't make a peep as they cleaned up and went to bed, and all the lights in the house were out.

Sing put his pipe out and set it on a chair when he saw a lantern approaching. Fen shuffled his feet over the dirt path, a wicked smile illuminated wretchedly by the lantern's flame.

Fen smiled and nearly shouted, "It is good to see you came out, Sing. Let's go find this Butterfly."

Words caught in Sing's throat and he looked back to the window which would lead into his bedroom. He thought he could see Jao, watching, waiting for his decision. He looked away, head downcast, and started walking. Any words he tried to conjure stuck in his throat.

Fen wouldn't stop talking about how glorious he imagined the Butterfly to be. He spoke of silk hair and porcelain skin, jade eyes and heavy breasts, and all other manner of inviting features. Sing knew his friend had never seen the woman before, and all the ideas were heady wishes of a man simply lusting for recreation. Sing didn't lust for another woman, but for sons. The woman was little more than a vessel to answer prayers and create dignity. To Fen, she was the prayer.

Sing pleaded with himself, tears silently dripping down his face unnoticed by his wanton friend. Why couldn't Sing just be happy raising the children he already had, growing old with his loving wife? She would sacrifice her life for the small possibility of a son. How could Sing think of sacrificing his faithfulness to his wife?

Sing was about to turn back when there were lights in the distance for a shack with rice paper walls, red-stained wood beams, and a red tile roof. Fen said, "We are here." The man moved swiftly over the final distance, and Sing struggled to keep up.

Once inside, red lacquered stairs led down into a tunnel. The stairs were eventually absorbed into the earth. The path went for some ways, though Sing was unable to tell how far they had traveled. The dirt smelled musty, and there was a cold dampness in the air, despite summer weather outside.

Sing and Fen reached a cavern not even the size of Sing's meagre home. At the entrance to the cavern was a man staring forward blankly until his gaze fell upon Sing and Fen. He asked, "Who are you?"

Fen laughed, "Tang, we thought you died. When did you come here?" Fen patted the man's shoulder. Tang was a villager, one Sing knew fairly well. Tang's wife and daughters were found in his house, which had burned down in the middle of the night. The husband and his three sons were never seen again.

Tang pushed Fen back. "Who are you? Queen Nabi isn't waiting for you."

Sing said, "Tang, you don't remember us? We would go to the market in Peng Ti. You enjoyed angering Fen, calling him a loveless lout." Fen grimaced at the memory.

Tang twitched, then tilted his head as if listening to something. After a tense moment, he said, "Come. Queen Nabi wants to see you." His voice was monotonous, with a slight buzz every time he spoke.

Fen puffed out his chest. "I knew we would be wanted."

Sing furrowed his brow. "Tang, why the change?"

Fen elbowed Sing, "Quiet. Don't ask questions. Soon her loins fill with our sons."

But there were so many questions, and with every tunnel traveled, more questions entered Sing's head. Men worked below the earth, moving soil around, building new passages, and solidifying what had already been burrowed. The men did their work without noticing Fen or Sing, and they were nearly all from the village. The first few men Fen tried to say hello, but there was no recognition in their eyes. They didn't even respond to sound.

"It's dark, that's why they don't know us," Fen rationalized for the question Sing had not asked. It comforted Sing some small degree to know Fen wasn't entirely without doubts, even if he could brush them aside.

"We should leave," Sing said.

Tang didn't turn around when he spoke. "No. We are almost there. After you meet her, you may leave."

Deeper in the tunnel there were young boys of all ages. Some Sing recognized, but many of the boys were new. Sing asked, "Where did the boys come from?"

"Queen Nabi only has boys," Tang said. The woman had been in town a few months, yet these boys were nearly teenagers.

The men entered a large cavern with natural pillars on either side of a long corridor leading to a throne hewn from the rock. On the rock sat a beautiful woman with purple hair which shimmered as the wings of an insect would. Her skin was pale. Black eyes peered out at the two men. Below her right eye was a tattoo of a purple butterfly. A dress wrapped around her lithe body tightly, like a cocoon, the fabric shimmering and flowing easily along her flat form. The stories certainly were lies, but they were more believable than the truth.

When Sing finally stopped gawking at the woman, it was as if Tang hadn't even been there. Fen was still enthralled with the Butterfly. She spoke, her voice laced with the same buzz as Tang had. "Two more workers for my little colony? Come, come." She gestured with her hands, and the two men dutifully walked forward. "Need to get a good look at you. Tang's eyes are so old. Hard to see through them." It felt like an instant between Sing starting to walk towards her and when he was in front of her, despite it being a few dozen paces.

"I am Queen Nabi of the far East." The voice resonated in Sing's skull, buzzing and vibrating pleasantly. It made it difficult to focus his eyes as they wanted to roll up. "I want a perfect world, and I will start with this village and this little colony. The men have been so kind and eager to help my vision." A finger caressed Sing's shoulder, went behind his neck, then traced a nerve up his neck and behind his ear. He shivered. She whispered in his ear, "Who are you two?"

Fen answered, "I'm Fen. I heard you give sons."

"Only sons. You have none? Or do you tire of your wife?" Despite speaking to Fen, she concentrated on Sing.

"You're far more beautiful. You are a gem next to the rock which burdens me."

"She must be truly a boring sight. What of you?" She moved so close that her nose touched Sing's. While waiting for an answer, and without looking away from Sing, she reached out for Fen with one thin, long finger, and gently touched his forehead with a lengthy nail. Fen's eyes went wide.

Sing choked on his words, intoxicated by the Butterfly's attention. "I am Sing. I want sons. I still love my wife greatly, though you are a very attractive young woman." He stepped back from the intimate space they shared and bowed, hoping it was the right thing to do. She was a queen, after all. Even more than that, he needed distance.

"So you are faithful except in shame. Then truly you've no sons." She tilted her head and gave a sad smile, a smile perhaps the spider gave to the caught fly out of pity. Both lived out of necessity, but one had to be sacrificed for the other to prosper.

"The ancestors and gods haven't seen it fit to give me a son yet." Sing kept his head down, staring at his feet. Maybe the Butterfly would simply disappear if he looked away, or that any moment Jao would wake him up from a fitful sleep.

The woman laughed, "And polite? I hope you see my future and understand. So few men as you come to my hive." She reached out with her finger, and Sing flinched. Making a tsk sound, she shook her head. "Do not fear the one you will call queen, my honey bee. This will not hurt." Sing closed his eyes until he felt the gentle finger nail against his brow. Then it started to pierce his skull, creeping into the space behind his eyes, and his eyes were opened.

Nabi spoke, but Sing could barely hear the words. Instead he saw a world in front of him. Great battles shed countless streams of blood. Heartbroken lovers wept and flung themselves from cliffs. Brothers killed each other for their inheritance. Wives were abused for birthing daughters. Baby girls were bashed against rocks. Sing fell to his knees and tears streamed down his cheeks.

Then there was a great swarm of butterflies leaving behind a purple haze. Wings swatted away the horrors of the world until all the images were gone. New images took shape. Men worked side by side creating great buildings, planting abundant fields, and bowing before their beloved queen. Each colony had a queen. Each queen had a harem. The queens only gave birth to sons, and there was no shame. Queen Nabi gave order and purpose to men. The world work without dissonance. It was the Heavens visiting earth with perfection.

The images faded, rippling apart until Sing saw what was in front of him: his queen. The world made sense. Her vision would create a land of harmony, without pain or heartache. There would be no shame, no desire beyond what one had, and everyone would be perfectly suited for their station. It only required following this woman obediently. Fen continued to stare ahead and whispered, "I understand."

The bliss was interrupted by visitors as Dian and his wife entered the cavern. Dian's wife, Mu, was sobbing, but she didn't fight against her husband. She was obedient to Dian as Dian was obedient to Queen Nabi.

Dian said, "I'm ready."

Queen Nabi nodded and two men came into the room. One escorted Dian to a room, and the other took away Mu. Queen Nabi smiled and said to Fen and Sing, "Return to me tomorrow." The two men left without an escort, knowing instinctively how to exit the tunnels.

Whispers swept the town the following morning. It didn't take long for Fen to rush to Sing, "It's Dian's wife. They found Mu dead in the fields. Dian is missing. You know what we have to do."

Sing looked to the ground. He should have been surprised, or at least shocked, but he knew what was happening. He straightened himself and said, "No. We have to do nothing." He could feel the image of perfect fields and families reach inside him and try to change his mind, but Jao and the girls anchored his heart.

"Go there again tonight. I will show you freedom." Fen grabbed Sing's arm, but Sing shrugged him off.

"I will not go to her again."

"You want sons. Sons will bring order to everything. Meet me there tonight." Fen started laughing as he ran off.

Sons would mean order. Sing looked towards his house and his eyes watered. Sons would end the shame of failing his ancestors.

That night, Sing did not return home. He went to see Queen Nabi once his daily chores were finished. He saw the visions and saw the order they brought. He desired it more than he desired sons.

When he arrived in the cavern, Fen's three unmarried daughters and his one son were already in the room with Queen Nabi. The girls were scared, whispering to each other and holding one another tightly. The boy was vacant, staring off into the distance.

Queen Nabi smiled at Sing. "Welcome home, dear." Then she went to the first girl and looked to Sing. "Do you know why I'm doing this?" She grabbed the first girl by the head, snapped it, and let her body slump to the floor. Sing's mouth dropped, but he couldn't find the words. "Order, my sweet. That's why. I want this world to make sense."

She went to the second daughter and thrust her nail into the girls head, between the eyes. The girl made a muffled thud against the dirt. "Women, so many of them, cause men to do such foolish things. Without so many women, men would have never come to me. Men wouldn't feel the shame of not having a son or the lust of wanting a more desirable woman. If only one woman, if that woman can control men, then there is no chaos, but order. That is why the gods are here, my dear. We wish to see the world elevated to order instead of shattered by chaos."

The youngest daughter let out a scream and fled, interrupting the monologue. Queen Nabi shook her head, "Little girl, there is nowhere to go. Your father gave you to me." The woman reached out with a hand and, starting with her index finger, began to morph into a swarm of butterflies which flew down the girl's mouth, until not a single butterfly was left. The girl fell to her knees, crying and convulsing in the dirt, reaching out as if some ancestor or god would save her. It did her no good, as the gods were in on it.

She crumpled, limp, to the ground. Sing shuddered. He desired to save the girl. When he looked at the girls face again, he saw Min's face, his daughter choking and dying.

A single purple butterfly left the girl's mouth, reforming into Nabi. "The ritual is ready. Follow me, and I will show the gateway to perfection."

They walked into a chamber with a floor steeped in the ruddy brown of dried blood. Fen's wife was restrained on a table with Fen standing over her, holding a knife. Fen looked up at Queen Nabi and smiled. His voice was raspy, "I'm ready to prove my love for my queen. To gain my sons."

Fen's wife begged. She pleaded to allow her to bear more children, and they would be boys. She asked what of their son, he did not need another. Fen's eyes glassed over and every word seemed silent to his ears. Sing knew sons were not the problem, and a woman could not make her body younger or more desirable. There was no removing a man's superficial lust when his heart was set on it.

Nabi smiled at Sing, "They all have a choice. I don't do what my brethren do, stripping free will entirely. Order appeals to people. They love the chance to be told what to do no matter the cost. You and I know Fen is not here for sons. He is here for a beautiful face which will never age. A young body which will never disappoint. I can give that, and so he will sign himself away to me."

Nabi nodded to Fen. He slashed across his wife's throat, then buried it in her heart as she gurgled. He dug around with the blade for a time before drinking of the pulsing river gushing from her chest. Her heart's blood. A thing of curses.

Fen's wife went silent, the writhing body becoming still. Fen looked up, her blood splashed across his face and chest. "I prove my love for you, my queen. Take me."

Sing vomited and ran. He knew of many bridges he would cross for a son, but watching his daughters die and killing Jao was not such a bridge. To see how far his friend would fall for the taste of a young body disgusted him.

He tumbled through the tunnels, tripping on people and stumbling into walls, but his feet never stopped. The walls felt like they were closing in on him as he heard a buzz fill the underground dwellings. The men doing work stopped and watched. Some of them started to move towards Sing, but they were addled and their hands could not grasp him. Many had difficulties running.

He burst through the doors of the shack and was out in the open field. The fresh air felt good in his burning lungs, though Sing never stopped running. The moon was high enough to give some sense of direction, but the man still tripped on the uneven land. His mind raced, his heart felt as if it were to explode in his chest. Sing loved his wife and daughters. He loved his family and what they had become. He could live with the shame of no sons. He could live with the chaos of raising those girls for another family, leaving him to work all his life. He could not live without the woman he married and the daughters he sired. He loved them, and the gods and ancestors provided them for a reason.

Then he was home, running into the door with enough force to rip it off the hinges. He tumbled across the floor on shattered wood. Soon Jao was in the room, "Sing, what...?"

"Get the kids. Get some food and clothes. We have to run."

"Why?" She helped her husband up, and he went to the children, pulling out the three girls. He carried Diao and pushed

Ling and Min into the common room. The two girls rubbed sleep from their eyes, groaning and complaining. Sing told them all to hush and grab dry food.

The girls grabbed the food and Jao put it in sacks. Diao was crying. Sing caught his breath and said, "I saw the Butterfly. She kills all the women to give men sons. I don't want sons. I want you all to live." Jao stared at Sing, featureless, and Sing felt guilty. "When we reach another village, you can claim you do not know me. I do not deserve you."

"Foolish man. I am your wife. You are still beside me." Jao stood and wrapped the sack around her torso. She grabbed the girls by the hand, and the family fled the house. In the distance, buzzing filled the air.

It was sunrise. Behind them, a black cloud started to close in. In front of them, the sun broke the horizon. There were figures off in the distance, armed men and women. Sing shouted, "Help!" The man's lungs were on fire and his vision started to narrow. "Please, Help!"

The small band of a half dozen made their way to Sing and his family. A man with white hair asked, "What's wrong?"

Jao said, "A god is controlling the men of our village. She is behind us in the sky." Jao said it with a straight face, though when Sing heard the words, he couldn't imagine anyone believing the tale.

The white-haired man nodded. "Our rogue." The swarm closed in and the man crooked his index finger and blew through it. Winds gusted across the field, kicking up dust. When the dust settled, the swarm was gone. The man said, "There is a town three days down that road. Go there and say Lu Shuan sent you. They are kind." The band went ahead, towards the self-proclaimed queen.

Sing caught his breath and stood, "Our ancestors watch us today. We will start over."

Jao bowed and hugged her husband, "So they are. May they ever remain kind." So the family headed towards the new village to start their new life, Sing no longer ashamed of his blessings.

FOUR FACES OF DORIAN GRAY

BY S. F. GEBEL

The tapping of the pen on paper was soothing, like the ticking hands of a clock. I refused to keep a clock in my office, as I believed it prevented people from paying attention to the present. They were always fixated on time. Time passed. Time wasted. Time left.

To be honest, I did not actually know what time it was. I could not even remember what day it was, or how I had arrived here.

I dropped the pen, looking up when the staccato knocking started, revealing Greta's grim appearance.

She was dressed in dark jeans, knee-high black boots, a black long-sleeved shirt, and a black hoodie, hood up.

"Morning Greta," I said, motioning for her to take the seat in front of me.

She removed her sunglasses as she walked to the leather armchair.

"Hello," she said, sitting down and crossing her right leg over her left, placing both her hands on either armrest.

"How are you feeling today?" I asked, overlooking her eye roll.

She tilted her head to the side and stared at me, challenging me to come up with a better question, one that deserved a response.

I could see the flecks of gold in her hazel eyes. Those flecks were the last evidence of the passionate person she used to be.

Two months ago Greta buried her mother. She had been dying of breast cancer for almost seven years, but it wasn't the tumours that killed her. It was the drunk driver.

Greta's sudden personality shift after her mother's funeral led her to counselling, led her to me.

"I thought today we could talk about coping," I said, leaning forward. "In order to prevent the grief from taking over, we have to find a way to cope with the loss. I know you and your mother were very close, and I'm sure watching her slowly die was difficult, and then to have her pass so suddenly. That must have been a shock."

I paused for a response, but all I got was a shift in posture. Greta sat up straighter and leaned to the right, resting her head on her closed fist.

"I know part of what makes death so hard is that we relive it daily. We always miss those gone, but what you have to remember is your mother's in a better place. She's at peace and no longer in pain. She will always be watching over you and can remain alive through you."

Greta opened her fist, placing her middle finger over her top lip, and her pointer finger on her cheek.

I thought I saw crescent indents on her palm. Nail marks.

"I know when my grandmother died, I felt lost, and I was convinced the sadness would never go away. It did, in time. It's still present, and it always will be, but I've learned to live with the sadness, and so will you."

Greta's shoulders rose as she took a deep breath.

Perhaps comparing my grandmother to her mother was not the best idea.

She breathed out through her nose, as the fingers on her left hand tapped the armrest.

"I've talked with your friends, colleagues, and even your aunt and uncle; none of them believe that you've properly grieved.

They say you haven't cried, you haven't talked to anyone, and they feel you might be in denial." I said, interlacing my fingers as I looked at her. "After the few sessions we've had I don't believe you're in denial. You understand what has happened and you've accepted it. That being said, my concern is that you only internalize your grief. You have to let it out somehow or it will consume you. You have to find a way to move passed this point and start the healing process. Your mother would want you to be happy."

I saw her left hand wrap around the armrest as her right leg began to shake, the heel of her boot pounding into the floor.

"When someone is dying of cancer we start to anticipate the end, to think we can prepare ourselves for the inevitable, but we can't. I also know that many times people grieving try to find the meaning in death. They try to understand why something happened the way it did, or why it happened at all. You have to let go of trying to understand why, because that road only leads to more suffering. It's a double-edged sword: the desire to end it quickly or make it last as long as possible. You're conflicted because you don't really know how you feel, and your feelings change daily. You feel like there's no escape, but there is."

Greta's throat constricted as she swallowed. She was looking directly at me, but I still felt like she wasn't listening.

I took my own deep breath as I continued. "I know your mother was a religious woman, and so I hope it gives you comfort to know that she's with God, and that he's with you, too. God never gives us more than—"

Greta stood up, knocking her chair over, turning to leave.

"OK," I said, standing up and running to block her path. "I shouldn't have said that, I'm sorry. Please, I'm just trying to help."

Greta looked up at me, shaking her head as she turned around. She stopped halfway as she saw the picture next to my bookshelf.

The painting was of a young man, no more than twenty. His chin-length hair was a golden brown framing the contours of his face, matching the colour of his arched eyebrows, which sat atop dark brown eyes. One could not help but stare at this young man, whose sculpted features contained a chiseled chin, high cheekbones, pointed nose, and skin as pale and smooth as steamed milk. The only colour came from the lips, like stained wine, with the corners rising in an omniscient smirk. His neck was barely visible above a white collared shirt that rested on a charcoal grey suit, finished off with a pink rose pinned above the heart.

"Dorian Gray," Greta said.

I stood next to her, watching her face as she stared at the portrait. She was smiling. Not a happy smile, but an appreciative smile.

"How tragic," she said.

I quickly turned off the music when I saw his face peering through the crack in my door. "Come in Roger," I said as I beckoned him to join me.

"Do you want the door opened or closed?" He asked, standing awkwardly by the door, not quite in the room.

"Whatever you're comfortable with," I said.

Every time I saw him I was unnerved by his composure. His face was void of emotion, but covered in lines and age spots, like an etch-a-sketch that couldn't fully erase anymore.

It had taken me almost all of our first session to understand why he was here. At first I had presumed he was a man whose over-the-hill age justified his weary face, but on realization as to how the face had become so serious, I decided that just maybe, he needed me more than he knew.

Roger was going on five years of divorce and thirty years of reflection.

He took his time walking to the chair; an old football injury to the right knee had left him with a permanent limp. The cloudy weather outside was not helping.

"How's the leg?" I asked.

"Hurts to drive. Hurts to walk. Just hurts," Roger said, slouching slightly as he stretched out his leg, rubbing the kneecap.

"Still refuse to take anything for the pain?" I asked.

"I like the pain," Roger said, still rubbing his knee.

"Explains why you like talking about it," I said.

"Pain is a physical reminder of the past," Roger said.

"Pain hinders your ability to live in the present," I said.

We had this same conversation each session. Nothing changed. He was set in his ways.

"My sister is not paying you so we can talk about my knee," Roger said, finally sitting up to look at me.

"She's worried about you," I said. "She believes you're depressed and is concerned about what could come from that depression. Particularly since you live alone and don't get out much."

"I get out every day," Roger said, interlacing his fingers across his chest, elbows resting on either side of the chair.

"Aside from work you only get out to meet me for an hour every Wednesday. That does not count," I said, sighing. "I know you're an introvert. I know you like peace and quiet, but I also know that you have closed yourself off from the world and I'd like to know why."

"The world doesn't want anything to do with a crotchety nobody like me," Roger said.

"Maybe the world could learn something from you," I said. "You've lived, Roger."

"You telling me because you think I don't remember?"

"No, I think all you do is remember. You do nothing but remember the past and what you've been through, but you need to remember that you're alive in the present and you need to focus more on your future. You act like nothing matters."

"I'm not suicidal," Roger said.

"I never said you were."

"People always seem to think I am," Roger said.

"When someone reacts to life-changing events by closing themselves off from the rest of the world, it tends to make those who care about them nervous." I said, sliding my chair back to come stand in front of him. "Don't you want to create new memories rather than hide out in old ones?"

"I know how the old ones end," Roger said, his words barely audible. I don't think he had intended to speak.

"What do you mean?" I asked. "You hide out because the future is so uncertain?"

"No, I—" Roger stopped, staring directly into my face. "You think you're so smart because for a brief moment two weeks ago I let slip that I was plagued by regret—"

"You didn't let anything slip, Roger," I said. "I have no idea what you regret. Is it how your marriage ended? Is it that your father died while you were traveling through Europe and you weren't there? Is it that your mother died while you two weren't speaking? I want to help you, but you're inside your head, and have closed it off so no one else can see in."

"No one else needs to bother," Roger said. "I can handle my own problems."

"Obviously not," I said, crossing my arms as I leaned back on my desk.

"I'm sure you're very nice, but I don't know you and I don't trust you." Roger said, scooting his chair back.

"You have to trust someone," I said.

"I don't trust anyone."

"Why?" I asked.

"I can't trust someone else when I don't trust myself," Roger said, standing up, his arm reaching for the back of the chair as his knee gave out.

"Why don't you trust yourself?" I asked, noticing we were on the verge of a breakthrough.

"I've made poor decisions, which at the time I thought were good, but I've now come to wish I'd done things differently. But since you can't change the past, you're stuck being reminded of what you did wrong. Since I don't want to have any more regrets, I think it's best if I don't take any more chances."

We stood staring at each other for a few minutes. He was

waiting to see what I said and I was trying to think of what to say.

I could only think of one thing to say. "Each man lived his own life, and paid his own price for living it. The only pity was one had to pay so often for a single fault."

"Excuse me?" Roger asked.

"It's from The Picture of Dorian Gray," I said, pointing to the painting.

"Francine?" I said into the waiting room.

"Down here," a soft voice said.

I looked down to my left to see her sitting in the corner between the chairs. Her curly brown hair was pulled back in a butterfly clip, while her knees were tucked under her blue dress. One book was open on her lap, while the remaining was stacked at her feet.

"What are you reading?" I asked, reaching for her hand to help her up and grabbing the stack of books so she could grab her backpack.

Rather than answer she held up the book so I could read the cover, The Secret of the Old Clock.

"You like Nancy Drew?" I asked, noticing the other three were the same series.

"I like solving mysteries," Francine said as she followed me into my office. "It's satisfying to figure out the end before it happens."

"You like knowing all the answers?" I asked, turning around when she didn't respond. "Francine?"

"Call me Cinny," she said, the words coming out slowly as she stared off to the side.

I followed her trajectory. She was transfixed on him.

When I looked back at her I noticed her shifting from side to side, only a couple of steps in either direction.

"His eyes follow me," she said.

"I can take him down if you—"

"I like him," she said.

"You do?"

"I feel that as long as he's staring I have to tell the truth. He won't let me get away with anything." Cinny said, her head turning to face me. "You know the eyes are the windows into the soul?"

"I've been told," I said. "Shall we sit?" I started to kneel but stopped as she came to stand next to me.

"I want to sit on this side," she said, still staring at the portrait.

She would keep Dorian in her sights at all times.

We both sat on the rectangular rug where I'd placed several games and colouring books.

"What would you like?" I asked, gesturing to the assortment as I noticed her hands moving up and down her arms, lost without a book to hold.

She pulled the Rock 'Em Sock 'Em game in between us.

"Do you find comfort in knowing the answer?" I asked, trying to bring us back to our original conversation.

"It's not that I need to know the answer. I just need to know an answer." She said, putting her fingers on the controls. "Uncertainty annoys me."

"That's why you enjoy reading books and watching movies, because you learn how everything ends?"

"I know how everything ends. The end is always the same no matter the journey," she said.

She did not have to say it. I knew exactly what she meant. Death.

She looked up at me and in that moment she did not look like she was nearing 12. She looked no more than eight.

Fear reversed the aging process.

"Do you fear the end?" I asked, deciding not to say the word out loud.

"My father had a heart attack last month," Cinny said.

"And you thought he was going to die?" I asked.

"He was dead," she said. "He had the heart attack in front of me. He fell to the ground and he wasn't breathing. I kept shaking him and screaming for help. He stayed unconscious until the paramedics arrived. I thought my father was dead for 10 minutes."

"That must have been so scary," I said.

"It was so terrifying that I felt nothing," she said.

"Excuse me?"

"I think that when a person feels something so strongly so quickly that it shuts them down and they end up feeling nothing at all. It's like a computer that overheats and fries itself. They cannot handle what is happening as it is too overwhelming and they are unable to compartmentalize the situation because it happens so fast. All a person can do is shut down, go numb, because that is the only way they know how to survive without falling apart. Unfortunately, when the event is over and everything appears to be fine that doesn't mean they can flip a switch and return to who they were before it happened. They continue to be numb, and those around them interpret it as unfeeling."

She stopped to take a breath and her fingers pressed the controls so her robot punched the other one. She repeated that a few more times before continuing. "When I was waiting for the paramedics I did not feel scared or sad or angry or worried. The only thing I felt was alone."

I took longer to speak then I wanted to. "Do you still feel alone?"

"I'm always alone," Cinny said. "It's not just that I'm an only child, but I realize now that when my parents die I will be the only one left. I'll be the sole keeper of the memories and feelings. No one else will know. No one else will understand, not really." She said, her voice rising as if the fear became more tangible with each word. "Is there anything scarier than the feeling of finality? The feeling of loneliness? The feeling of having no control over the inevitable, over your own life?"

"You are in control of your own life, Cinny," I said, pushing the game aside so she could focus solely on my words. "You can control how you feel about what has happened, what is happening, and what will happen. You're facing your fears right now. All you have to do is defeat them. Be stronger than your fears."

I swallowed two Aleve with half a glass of water. I always had a headache by the end of the day.

I jumped out of my chair when I heard pounding at the door. "Come in," I said.

The door opened to reveal a young man no more than twenty. He was wearing low-ride jeans, scuffed boots, and a jean jacket over a black shirt with a faded ACDC symbol. I noticed a tattoo on the side of his neck, but couldn't make out the image. I could, however, clearly see his pocketknife.

"Take a seat, Adam." I said, nodding to the chair across from me.

"I don't think I will," he said, boots scraping against the floor as he walked forward, leaning against the back of the chair.

"You can stand if you feel more comfortable," I said, leaning back slightly so he wasn't so close. "Do you understand why you're here?"

"Court order for anger management," Adam said, flinging the chair across the room so it smashed against the cabinets. "I think they're overreacting."

"Do you feel better now that you've destroyed something?" I asked, standing up. He still towered over me.

"You don't know what you're dealing with," Adam said. "I don't like being told what to do. I don't like others thinking they know better than me, or worse, that they know me."

"So you've decided to hate me before even meeting me? You've decided that the best way to deal with forced anger management is to remain angry?"

"Can't a guy just be angry without everyone trying to calm

him down?" Adam asked, arms crossed.

"As long as that anger doesn't cause harm," I said, looking at my fallen chair.

"Let's just get this over with," he said. "I don't want to be here. You don't want me here, but at least you're getting paid."

"Can you at least tell me why you're so angry?" I asked, leaning against the wall.

"You can't understand," he said.

"Try me."

"Invisible father, abusive mother, and working three jobs just to afford the car, food, and clothes that allow me to work three jobs."

Adam's eyebrows rose as he dared me to respond.

"I'd be angry too," I said. "However, I know from experience that the anger will eat away at you until there's nothing left."

"What do you suggest I replace my anger with?" Adam asked, placing the palms of his hands on my desk.

"I suggest you release your anger in a constructive and therapeutic—"

Before I could finish Adam used his right arm to dump the contents of my desk onto the floor. I heard the pens rattle in their ceramic cup before it shattered.

I took a deep breath. My mother had given me that cup.

"Feels pretty therapeutic to me," Adam said, a crooked smile plastered on his face.

I noticed a scar on the left side of his chin. It was an oval, caused by opening up from continuous movement. It was years old, but had not properly healed.

I moved to stand in front of my bare desk to prevent him from throwing it across the room too. "I am not going to be intimidated by your behaviour. You want to be angry, fine, but figure out exactly what you're angry at, because until you do you will continue to be angry at everything."

"Misplaced anger," Adam said, turning away from me. "That's what you've come up with. Brilliant deductive skills."

"Why are you angry?" I asked again. "It's a simple question."

"What happens when I tell you?" Adam asked. "I give you an honest answer and you'll spout a simple solution to what you think is a simple problem. I need a better outlet for my aggression, but the problem is that when I'm angry is the only time people listen. Either because they are scared of me, scared for me, or just too damn uncomfortable with my honesty."

"You think you're an honest person?" I asked.

Adam shrugged his shoulders and twitched his head in response.

"You want honesty?" I asked, pushing myself off of my desk. "Your outbursts of rage and constant need to yell might make you feel better, briefly, but the source of the anger never goes away and soon you're mad again. All you succeed in doing is making everyone around you miserable, which makes you feel worse. Wouldn't you rather just stop?"

"Wow," Adam said, raising his eyebrows and shaking his head. "Just like that you think you have me all figured out. You think that my anger means I'm an open book for you to judge in your superiority. Therein lies the problem."

"Which is?"

"The world is made up of hypocrites, like you," Adam said.

"I'm a hypocrite?" I asked.

"The worst part is you don't even realize it. You advise me based on some moral compass you think I lack. You believe you know better than me, because you're able to pass societal inspection. You look at me and see an angry young man, and you feel sorry for me. You want to help me to become more like you. What a load of crap!"

"I want to help you be better than you are, be more than an angry person who hates the world," I said.

"I don't hate the world," Adam said. "I just see it for what it really is."

"A world of phonies?" I asked, inhaling a few deep breaths.

"Exactly," Adam said. "You think you know more than everyone who comes through that door, because you have a handle on life. You think you're better than me because you're not constantly angry? Can you honestly tell me nothing bothers you? If you think that than you're lying to yourself."

Adam's eyes shifted to the portrait and back to me with a laugh. "You have a portrait of Dorian Gray and yet you don't realize you're trying to be him. You put on a face for the world to see, while making sure all the ugliness of life is hidden away. People who hide the truth, that's what angers me."

We stood staring at each other. He had finished saying all he had to, and I was trying to choose my words carefully.

"It's like talking to Holden Caulfield," I said under my breath as I turned to walk back behind my desk.

"He saw the world as it really was," Adam said, causing me to turn back towards him. He smiled at seeing the surprise on my face. "You thought I wouldn't get that reference?" He nodded his head before saying, "No one ever sees passed the anger."

I stood in front of the portrait, reflecting on Adam's words. He was right.

I was sad. I was regretful. I was scared. All of which made me angry.

I stared at Dorian's face and couldn't help but think that it was a lie.

I spent my whole life putting on a façade so that no one would know that deep down I was as screwed up as the rest of them. In fact, I was worse.

When I closed my eyes I saw it all. Everything I had done and everything I was doing, and I could no longer see where I was going.

Without thinking I raised my right arm and punched a hole through Dorian Gray's face.

I did not hear the rip of the torn canvas, but rather the sound of shattered glass.

I opened my eyes to see a woman's face, broken, fragmented

like the bathroom mirror.

My face.

Mid 20s with curly, brown hair turning silver at the roots, and hazel eyes hidden behind black glasses that magnified the gold flecks. Other physical features included an improperly healed scar on the left side of the chin, stiff limp in the right knee, and a bloody right fist.

I looked back up at my reflection in the shattered mirror, but did not recognize the person staring back.

CHANGELING

BY N. E. HARVEY

To whomever finds this note:

You probably already know my name. No doubt I am splashed all over the front page. They'll say "Loving Mother Kills Family after Psychotic Break" or something like that. Maybe they're right. Maybe I *am* crazy. All I know is that I have to do something to get rid of it.

I write this letter to you while watching my beautiful daughter playing with, for want of a better term, her identical twin. I bet that sounds weird to you, doesn't it? Why don't I just say I am watching my twin daughters play together?

Because I only have one daughter. I only have one child. I don't know what kind of creature is mimicking my little girl but I know I only gave birth to one baby. I *know* we only brought one child home with us. Whatever that thing is, wearing my daughter's face, I know it isn't mine. It's not even human. I'm sure of it.

When my husband and I found out that I was pregnant, we were over the moon. We'd been trying for five years with no luck and had almost given up hope when that little stick finally turned blue. We did everything we could to make sure my pregnancy ran smoothly, terrified that something would happen to ruin all our hopes and dreams but we needn't have worried. I had terrible morning sickness at the start, but after that I bloomed and everything was perfect. Absolutely perfect.

I went into labour at around midnight on my due day. Like I said - perfect. The pain was relentless, but just about bearable and it took only twelve hours from the first contraction to the birth. I gave birth naturally with only a little gas and air and I was allowed home the same day. David and I were full of joy. We felt so *complete*. Nobody can understand true happiness until they hold a child of their very own in their arms for the first time.

We named our beautiful daughter Evelyn because it means 'longed for'. Appropriate, right? I brought back the paperwork from the hospital and locked it in the old wooden box with iron edging my grandmother had given to me when I was a little girl. It looked like the briefcase my dad always took to work with him, only it was twice as deep and didn't have a handle.

"This box is special, dear. Don't ever forget it. It's made with iron, which the faeries can't touch. And these scissors on the top - they're to protect the contents. Everything important to you should be kept in this box. There are little magical faerie folk out there in the forest and they'll cause all manner of troubles if they can."

Dad said it wasn't real and faeries didn't exist, but I moved my prized possessions into that box anyway, just in case. As I grew older, the superstition died, but habit survived and I kept putting important things into that box. My favourite toys and hair ribbons gave way to ticket stubs, photographs and my driving licence in my teens, with my life insurance policy, passport and my favourite photos of David and I replacing those as I grew older. I had my ultrasound scans and baby shower gift tags all bundled up with ribbon and when my beautiful baby was born, naturally I added the birth certificate and a loose sheaf copy of my hospital records to my iron box of memories.

Everything stopped being perfect a few days after the birth. My husband, David, was asleep and I had just put Evelyn down after a late night feed. I collected my box from the bedroom and carried it downstairs to spend a few minutes looking back at my scans and Evelyn's first photos. Eventually I made myself put them away. I needed to get some sleep before my little angel woke again. I put everything back into the box, closed the lid carefully, locked it and traced the scissors on the top absently with my fingers.

Without warning my fingers became fused to the lid. I tried to pull away but they were stuck. I yelped as I tugged and pulled but it was no use. I could feel my heart pounding and my legs beginning to tremble.

As suddenly as they had become stuck, my fingers were freed and I fell to the floor, knocking over my chair with a crash. Instantly a cry sprang up from the nursery so I ran up the stairs to settle Evelyn down before she woke David up, examining my fingertips for any sign of damage as I went. As the door to the nursery swung open in front of me I froze. My baby was lying on the floor by the window. I could hear crying, but it was coming from inside the cot. I edged slowly across the floor, my eyes fixed on the cot as I moved closer. Another baby was bawling hungrily in the cot, looking right at me. I stared wordlessly, my gaze jumping back and forth between the two babies, my legs acting on autopilot, backing me away until my spine was pressed against the wall.

What is happening? I thought. *There are two. Why are there two?*

My husband found me frozen like a statue against the wall, one baby bawling in the cot and the other still peacefully slumbering on the floor.

"Eileen? What are you doing? Why is Aislinn crying? Why the hell is Evelyn on the *floor*?"

He scooped Evelyn off the floor and placed her into a second cot that I hadn't noticed, before picking up the other baby and attempting to soothe her. I just stared. Thoughts and questions flickering through my mind that I refused to grasp hold of, for fear I would lose it completely.

"We only have one baby." I mumbled, confused. I knew; I knew we only had one baby. I didn't know what was going on but I was sure we only brought home one baby.

"Darling what are you talking about?"

I folded my arms across my chest, I felt lost. I felt like my entire world was an alien place.

"Evelyn is our daughter but there was no other baby. I should know; I'm the one that carried and gave birth to her."

David rubbed the tips of his fingers against his forehead as he huffed out a breath in a sigh.

"Eileen, it's late. You need sleep. Let's talk about this tomorrow. Okay? You're probably exhausted or something. I don't know. We'll go see the doctor. Okay?"

"I... okay." I sighed, giving in. I *was* exhausted. I followed David out of the now quiet nursery and curled up in bed, my thoughts sluggish as sleep slowly claimed me. I couldn't have forgotten one of my babies, could I? I'd been so desperate for a family.

The next day, David took me to the hospital and I was shown my hospital records. In it were records of a twin pregnancy and a twin birth. Aislinn had apparently been born 20 minutes after Evelyn. By all accounts it had been a challenging birth - Aislinn almost didn't survive. They thought maybe my mind had blanked it out because I couldn't handle remembering such a harrowing ordeal. I still had no memory of her before that night; no matter how much "evidence" I was provided. Eventually I was put on medication and offered counselling for trauma and postpartum depression. I also had to deal with regular visits from social services "just to make sure you are managing okay and don't need any additional help". What they actually did is make me feel watched. Judged.

I tried.

I swear, I really tried to find it in me to love Aislinn but I can't.

I just can't love her.

She isn't mine.

No matter what David says, or the hospital, or my therapist, she isn't mine. She can't be. I've been flushing my pills down the toilet each day so it looks like I've been taking them, but I'm not the one who has a problem. My little Evie is a delightful happy sunny baby. Aislinn is the opposite. No human baby is capable of manipulation the way she is. She's so much hungrier than Evelyn, more demanding. She eats and eats and eats and is never full. I caught her hitting Evie once when she thought I wasn't looking; she was swinging her arm back and into Evie's face over and over again. They were just five months old. I swear Aislinn feigns illness and cries and cries non-stop on purpose when the social services lady is here, just to keep us focused on her. I started deliberately focusing on Evelyn when social weren't around; handing Aislinn to David to feed, bathe and change as often as I could. She did not like that. Not at all.

David is besotted with Aislinn, so when he came home one

day to find her crawling along the kitchen counter, reaching for the knives in the knife block, he was beside himself with rage. He screamed at me for hours about how I must have put her up there and left the room, then challenged me when I insisted that's not what happened. I am *sure* she was in the play pen with Evelyn when I dozed off. There is no way she should have been able to get out the pen by herself, let alone get into the kitchen and up on the cabinets. She was meant to be a seven month old baby for crying out loud. I'd only noticed her crawling a few days earlier. Evelyn hadn't even managed that. Aislinn always seemed to learn to do things first. David slept in the spare room that night and when I went to find him in the morning, Aislinn was curled up next to him, looking at me with a knowing, satisfied smirk on what should have been an innocent baby's face.

That was the last time David and I slept in the same bed. He moved his clothes into the spare room the next morning.

"I think it's for the best until you begin to feel better. I'm moving Aislinn's cot too." He didn't add *so you can't get to her* but I could hear it in the awkward silence that followed instead. Aislinn was getting in the way of my marriage now.

As the weeks wore on, more unexplainable things happened and David grew more distant, hesitating before entering a room I was in and avoiding physical contact. He was working from home so he didn't have to leave Aislinn but she still managed to find a way to get the child lock off the cabinet containing the bleach in the kitchen, climb the front of the cabinet full of glasses in the dining room and knock my glass ornaments off the shelves with a resounding crash, and, it makes me shudder to say it, David kept finding her in my room whilst I was sleeping, playing with things like an old razor, a pair of scissors, and a metal nail file. I had no idea how she got hold of those things, but of course David blamed me. He accused me of not only being irresponsible, but of deliberately leaving dangerous things within her reach. He said I must have left them in the waste bin on the floor of the bedroom. I'd never do that. What if Evelyn picked one up?

I have another theory. Aislinn wants to kill me.

I tried to tell David but he just wouldn't listen. I guess I can't blame him; I wouldn't believe it either, but it's the only thing that makes sense. I wanted to open my grandmother's old box and prove to him that she wasn't mine. That the original paperwork proved that only Evelyn was our baby. That this imposter, this... *thing* was not our baby at all. I got the box down from on top of the wardrobe in what should have been mine and David's bedroom and took the key from the chain around my neck. As I inserted the key into the lock, a shudder ran through me, raising goose bumps on my skin and leaving me with a sense of foreboding. I looked up towards the door and there was Aislinn, her gaze locked on the box on the table, her little body tense with anticipation. As I took in the strange glint in her eye I felt a sudden urge to take up the box and run. That box holds all the proof I have. I couldn't let her work her voodoo on it like she has with everything else in my life. That box is my vindication. I put it away and, when she was finally asleep, I buried it in the garden among the roots of the apple tree. Inside, I hope, is proof that she is not my baby. That is really all the hope I have left and I urge you, reader of this note, to find it and prove that I was right about her.

Two hours ago, my world ended. David informed me that he was leaving me. Worse, he was taking Aislinn and Evelyn with him and taking me to court for full custody of them both, and the woman from social services was going to support his actions. I haven't even been a mother for a full year yet and I was deemed a failure. I begged and pleaded with him again, trying over and over to explain that Aislinn was the problem, that she wasn't our child. As always, he wouldn't listen. It just made him even more determined. Oh, how I'd love to never have to look at her again, but I couldn't handle losing Evie as well.

I can't cope with that.

Aislinn needs to go. Whatever kind of thing she is, masquerading as a sick copy of my little girl, she needs to be gone. I refuse to stop protecting what is precious to me and I do not want to be separated from my Evie.

Or David.

I don't know what else to do. It feels like this is the only option left to me. Evelyn, David and... that thing are all sleeping peacefully upstairs. I checked in on them before sitting down to write this letter. I'm going to leave it in David's car. Someone will find it eventually.

I am not crazy.

I am not making it up.

Aislinn is *not* my baby.

Proof is in my box. Please find it. I hope that it will allow for some forgiveness with what I am about to do. I can't let her be alone with Evie and David. He doesn't understand. She is dangerous; I feel it in my bones. I refuse to go to prison for getting rid of the evil creature though, and I refuse to lose David and Evie in the process.

I'm going to cut the gas lines in the kitchen and go to sleep, never to wake again. I believe that David, Evie and I will finally be a true family in heaven, whilst that thing suffers in hell for its trickery. That's the image I hold on to. That's what gives me the strength to do what must be done.

Forgive me.

Eileen Murphy

STAGES OF GRIEF

BY BECCA ODELIUS

It was an unseasonably cool Wednesday night in late June. I arrived in the parking lot a few minutes early and sat in my car staring at nothing. Deep breaths, I told myself. Don't start crying already.

A yellow Xterra pulled into the parking space next to me. I turned my head just enough to see the other driver in my peripheral vision. His hands still gripped the steering wheel at ten and two. I turned my head fully to get a better look at him. He was a slightly heavyset man, mid-thirties I guessed, with a thick head of hair and a few days scruff on his face. He stared straight ahead with a look of far away grief, and I suspected he was there for the same reason as I. The man got out of his car and glanced in my direction. Our eyes locked for a split second before he turned and slowly started toward the front doors of the church. If he can do this, so can I, I thought. One more deep breath... and go.

I walked into the building with shaking hands. My last visit to a church was my dead husband's burial, a day I tried to forget. I noticed a sign on an easel with the name of the bereavement group and an arrow pointing down a side hallway. The group met at the Lancaster Lutheran Church even though it didn't have any religious affiliation. I felt relieved we weren't meeting in the main sanctuary. I didn't need a crucified Jesus staring at me while I tried to put my grief into perspective.

The room where we met was small, intimate. The lights were dim, and the chairs were placed in a semi-circle with boxes of tissues under the seats. The man with the Xterra was already seated at one end. I took the empty chair across from him. He half smiled and nodded at me. I offered an awkward wave back. The room filled quickly. Some folks chatted lightly with each other at a table set up with coffee in the corner of the room. I sat quietly, fiddling with the strap of my purse. An older gentleman wearing a blue sweater and jeans entered and addressed the room.

"Hi, folks. If we could all find a seat. Let's get started," he said, grabbing a chair from against the wall and placing it at the front of the semi-circle. With a kind smile, he began the meeting. "I see a lot of familiar faces here. Frank, Sonja, nice to see you. Bob, hi. Alice? It's been awhile. Nice to have you back. To our new members, my name is Joe. I'm a certified grief counsellor and also a widower of ten years. I lost my wife, Ellen, to leukaemia right before our 25th wedding anniversary. To start off, let's go around the room and introduce ourselves, how we lost our spouses, and when it happened. If you'd like to share more, feel free. We are all here to help one another find a way to honour our lost loved ones as we learn to deal with our grief." Joe turned to the Xterra man. "Sir, would you like to begin?" The man cleared his throat and spoke.

"Um, my name is Garrett. I lost my wife, Kristy, on this most recent New Year's Eve to breast cancer. We have a daughter. Well, um, I have a daughter. Her name is Belle. Unfortunately, she witnessed her mother's decline with the cancer. Belle sat vigil by her mother's side, even at the very end when things got, well, difficult."

Many of us nodded, remembering the last days of our loved ones. Garrett looked around, seemingly relived that he didn't have to explain to any of us what he meant.

"Belle sees a therapist now, but her behaviour worries me. She talks about death and has these outlandish episodes where she

159

screams, cries, and makes herself vomit." Garrett paused and cleared his throat again. Then he continued slowly, "She's only nine. She'll be ten on Christmas Day." Another pause. "You know, they say holidays can be the best or worst day of your life. For me, it was both." One more clearing of the throat and a slight head nod let the group know he was done speaking. The woman next to him sniffled and put her hand on his shoulder. She already had a box of tissues ready on her lap. She spoke next.

"My name is Alice. I lost my dear partner, Mary, to lung cancer two years ago. We always hoped that one day we would be able to legally marry. I used to say to her, 'One day I will marry my Mary and be merry,'" she said as a slight sob escaped her lips. Garrett put his hand on her shoulder, a returned gesture of comfort for a grief that united us all.

By the time it was my turn, I almost lost my nerve. At first, I felt badly for Garrett because he had to go first. I decided going last was much worse. Every eye was on me as I began my story.

"My name is Charlotte. I lost my husband, Rob, this past October to colon cancer."

"Did you and your husband have any children?" one woman prompted me. I'm sure she meant to help me continue, but the question came at me so unexpectedly, it only made things worse.

I shook my head. My mind stalled, and I pleadingly looked at Joe to save me. Gratefully, he took the cue and began speaking to the group.

I stopped listening, though, too busy obsessing over that question. Why did other people assume it was their business to know if we had kids? And how could I tell them about the baby who expelled itself from my body two weeks after Rob's death? I was only three months along—the result of the last time Rob felt well enough to have sex. I had always wanted a child, yet Rob never felt ready, always a step behind. Granted, the thought of being a single mother scared me, but not nearly as much as the thought of being no one's mother. I shivered.

I quietly excused myself and found the women's restroom. I locked myself in a stall, sat down, and sobbed. I cried for the husband I lost and the baby I'd never know. I sat there for several minutes, thinking I should get back to the meeting, but the longer I stayed in the stall the more awkward I knew it would be to walk back into that room. I decided to go home.

As I slinked out of the bathroom, I noticed Garrett standing in the hallway. I looked around for another exit, but Garrett spotted me and walked toward me. I braced myself for an uncomfortable conversation.

"Hey," he said. "Charlotte, right?" I nodded. "Look, I saw you leave and wanted to make sure you're okay. I checked the parking lot and saw your car. I figured I could find you here. Not that I'm stalking you or anything, but..." His voice trailed off. Was he was trying to flirt with me? He ran his fingers through his hair, and I noticed he still wore his wedding band. I glanced down at the small rock on my left hand, and I knew he was just checking on me, like he said.

"Thank you." I said. "Garrett? Right? Look, the idea of therapy really isn't my thing. I'm not super comfortable around strangers, and being surrounded by them like this..." I shook my head, refocusing. "I'm only here because I got so tired of everyone in my life telling me how sorry they were with their looks of pity. I guess I thought that being around people who have been through what I've been through would be easier." I shrugged. "I don't know. Maybe I was wrong. God, I'm so embarrassed I just walked out like that." I glanced at my watch and realized the meeting would be over any minute. "I... I gotta get out of here. I'm sorry. Thanks for checking up on me. I'm okay. Really."

"Well, I'm not going back in there either," Garrett said. "Can I walk you to your car? I mean, we are parked right next to each other." I gave him a half-smile and nod. We walked together to the parking lot in silence.

"Okay, um, see ya," I said as I fished in my purse for my keys. Garrett cleared his throat.

"Listen," he began, "would you want to go grab a cup of coffee?" He quickly added, "Not like a date or anything! But, you know, I'm a pretty good listener. And maybe talking without a group of strangers staring at us would be beneficial for both of us." I considered turning down his proposal, but the thought of going home to an empty house, save for one very fat cat, was even less appealing.

"Yeah, okay," I finally said.

"Okay. Good. I'm just going to call the babysitter and let her know I'm going to be a little longer."

We drove separately to the diner down the street. The hostess sat us at a small table in the corner. It felt odd being somewhere with a man who wasn't my husband, but it didn't really feel like a date either.

"So, Charlotte," Garrett said as he took the menu from the hostess' hand, "is that like, Charlotte Brontë?" I let out a small snort. What a random question.

"Uh, no," I answered. "More like Charlotte, the city where I was born. I'm just grateful I wasn't born in Intercourse or some other unfortunately named town." I could feel a blush creeping up my neck as I silently chastised myself for sounding like a weirdo. Garrett chuckled.

"Interesting story about the little town of Intercourse," he said. "My wife, in her youth, stole the town's sign post while on a trip to Lancaster with her girlfriends." I laughed. Garrett laughed, too, but his grin quickly faded. "Kristy was crazy sometimes. She always wanted to go on these outlandish adventures. One time, when Belle was maybe two years old, Kristy wanted to hike the Appalachian Trail. As a family! It never happened, but I really wish she was still here so it could."

The waitress came over and we both ordered black coffee. I picked up the conversation where we left off.

"You want to hike the Appalachian Trail?" I asked.

"No," he admitted, "but I'd do it if it meant my wife was still with me."

"I know what you mean. There were things I never did that Rob wanted to do, but now, I'd do pretty much anything if it meant having him here." It surprised me how much talking to

Garrett really helped. I didn't feel as if he spent our conversation trying to figure out what he could say that wouldn't upset me like most people did.

Garrett's phone buzzed from the corner of the table. He glanced down at it.

"I'm sorry. It's the babysitter. I have to take this," he said to me. He answered, "Hello? Trina, what's up?" I watched Garrett's face as he listened to whatever the babysitter was telling him. He closed his eyes and let out a deep sigh. "Okay," he said into the phone, "I'll be right there."

"Is everything okay?" I asked after he hung up the phone.

"Unfortunately, no. Belle is vomiting all over the kitchen," Garrett said, while standing and pulling money out of his wallet.

"Oh no! I hope she'll be okay. Is there anything I can do?" Dumb question. What could I do? I felt like I should offer, anyway.

"No, no, but thank you. It's happened before. Her therapist believes it's from anxiety caused by losing her mother."

"Oh." A dumb response. What else could I say? Garrett threw a few dollars on the table, and we spent an awkward silence walking to the parking lot.

At our cars, Garrett was the first to speak. "Listen, Charlotte, this was really..." his voice trailed off as he moved his hands to help him come up with the right wording, "effortless, I guess I want to say. What I mean to say is it was good to talk to you."

I smiled and answered, "I couldn't agree more. Thank you, Garrett. I hope your daughter feels better soon. And thanks for the coffee."

"Thank you, Charlotte. Maybe I'll see you at next week's meeting?" I shrugged and got in my car to drive home.

The whole week after our visit to the diner I debated on whether or not I wanted to attend the next bereavement group. It was a lonely week interrupted only by six phone calls from my mother to check on me. By the time Wednesday rolled around, I decided to give group therapy another shot.

When I pulled into the church parking lot, I saw Garrett's

car. I felt less trepidation knowing there was a familiar face waiting inside.

The moment I walked into the room, I searched the small crowd for Garrett. I found him already seated, but he saw me and waved. Before I could make my way across the room, Alice, the grieving woman who sat next to Garrett the week before, caught me in an awkward embrace.

As she let me go, she said, "I'm so glad you came back, Charlotte! We were all worried about you. Don't you pay any mind to the nosey woman who asked you about having children. Even the grieving can be assholes sometimes. Mary and I didn't have kids. I mean, who would give two old lesbians a baby?" Alice laughed, but there was sadness in her eyes. I knew she was trying to make me feel better, so I thanked her and quickly escaped to claim the seat next to Garrett. I swallowed hard, last week's breakdown fresh in my mind. I tried to swallow the memory along with the lump in my throat.

"Hey, you okay, Charlotte?" Garrett asked as I sat down next to him.

"Yeah, I'm okay." Let's not talk about me. "How's your daughter? Is she feeling better?"

Garrett cleared his throat and nodded his head as he said, "Yeah, yeah. She's fine." He winced. "There was an episode at school this week."

"What happened?"

"She drew a pretty dark depiction of death in her art class. It apparently scared some of the other children. A few parents complained to the administration." He closed his eyes. "Every time I think she's learning to cope with Kristy's death, something like this happens. She just has a hard time being away from me, I think. I'm all she has left."

"Aw, poor thing!" I said.

Joe, our grief counsellor, walked in at that moment and asked the small crowd to take their seats. He introduced himself like the week before, and the meeting began. An hour later, I inwardly congratulated myself. I sat through the whole meeting without excusing myself to the bathroom. When it was over, Garrett asked if I wanted to get coffee again at the diner.

The hostess sat us at the same table in the same quiet corner. Garrett thanked her, and we both chuckled at the coincidence.

"So," Garrett began, "how was your week?"

"It was okay, actually," I said. "A little lonely. My mom called to check up on me." I paused and then added, "A lot." Garrett laughed and nodded. I continued. "I also have a cat who keeps me company. She's fat and lovable. Her name's Stella."

"Stellllllaaaaaaaaa!" Garrett joked.

"Exactly how I call her, too!" I said with a slight giggle. "She's a great cat. Rob gave her to me as a wedding present." My giggle faded. "She helps me miss him a little less, you know?"

"That makes sense," Garrett said. "Sometimes I can see Kristy in Belle's face. Especially when she smiles."

I reached across the table and offered a comforting squeeze to his hand. "That must be difficult for you."

"Sometimes, yeah," Garrett admitted. "But I feel fortunate to have a piece of Kristy with me. Even though Belle is going through a rough time right now, I can't imagine my life without her."

Garrett's phone buzzed exactly like it did the week before. "Speaking of Belle," he sighed. "It's the babysitter." Garrett answered the phone, "Hey, Elizabeth." Elizabeth? I thought her name was Trina?

A look of concern spread across his face. "Yeah, okay. Put her on." Garrett paused. "Hey, kiddo. Are you having a sad time?" Pause. "I'm just having coffee with a friend. Remember the woman I told you about who I met at the support group?" Another pause. "Soon. I'm leaving right now." Garrett closed his eyes and cleared his throat as he listened to his daughter on the other end. "I know, Sweetie. I miss Mommy, too. I love you. I'll see you in a few minutes."

Garrett took a deep breath as he hit the end button on his phone.

"Is there anything I can do?" I had no idea what it was like for him, but he looked so worried.

"I don't know what to do, Charlotte. I wish Kristy was here to help me, but then I remember if Kristy were here, we wouldn't have these issues," Garrett confessed. I reached out and laid my hand on his again.

"It sounds to me like you're doing everything you can do, Garrett. You seem like a loving, patient dad. I bet that's exactly what Belle needs right now," I said to him.

Garrett nodded. "Thanks, Charlotte. I needed to hear that." Garrett's voice cracked and, for a moment, I thought he was going to break down in tears. Instead, he cleared his throat and stood up. "So, we'll try again next week?" he asked.

"Absolutely."

The next week we did try again. And the week after that. Soon our coffee dates became dinner dates. We spoke less about our spouses and more about ourselves. We spoke less of the past and more about our futures. Only one thing remained the same: the phone call from the babysitter. I admired Garrett's patience and constant placing of his daughter first in his life. I think that's one of the reasons I began to fall in love with him.

The morning of one of our dates Garrett called me.

"Hi!" I said with a smile. "You aren't calling to cancel on me, are you?"

"Well, not exactly. The Xterra isn't starting and I need to take it the shop. Would you be okay with picking me up tonight?" he said, but he sounded nervous.

"Sure. That's not a problem." I prodded. "Is everything else okay?"

"Well," he began, "I was thinking you might want to come inside and meet Belle." I heard the familiar sound of Garrett clearing his throat.

"Oh." I wasn't sure how I felt about that. It seemed like the natural next step in our relationship, but kids didn't always like me. And I wanted Belle to like me. To do that, I realized I'd have to meet her eventually. Still... "Okay, I think that would be nice," I finally said.

I arrived at Garrett's house a little before seven. I checked my makeup in the visor mirror and took a deep breath. I smiled at myself, trying to trick my face into masking my frazzled nerves.

I grabbed the gift I brought for Belle off the passenger seat and made my way up the sidewalk to the front door. When I rang the doorbell, I could hear the screaming of a child's voice. It was shrill and constant. I stood frozen, not sure what to do.

Garrett opened the door and stood there looking frazzled.

"Hey, Charlotte. Come on in. Just give me a sec, okay?" He turned his head and yelled, "Belle! Get down here!"

"Nooooooooooooooo!" came a child's reply. The babysitter stood in the doorway of the kitchen. She looked absolutely terrified. Garrett excused himself and disappeared up the stairs.

"So," I said to the babysitter, "I guess you're probably used to this by now."

"I don't know," the teenage girl responded. "This is my first time babysitting her."

"Oh," I said. "Well, I'm sure it will be fine!" I tried to reassure the young girl but had no idea what the night held. Garrett came back downstairs with a very unhappy looking nine year old. Belle hid behind her father and peeked at me with a face of utter disgust.

Even with her scowl, she was clearly a beautiful child: tall for her age with dark curls that framed her oval face. Her brown eyes were like daggers, and they pierced my confidence to a frightening point.

"Belle," Garrett said, "say hello to Charlotte."

A muffled reply came from the folds of Garrett's shirt.

"Hi, Belle," I said carefully. "It's so nice to meet you. Your dad has told me so much about you!" She didn't move from behind her father, so I kept trying. "I heard you like to read. I brought you a present." I held out the copy of Charlotte's Web. "Have you ever read this book? It was one of my favourites when I was about your age." Belle took the book from my hand and looked at me.

"I've read it," Belle said. "I like the end when Charlotte dies." She gave me a cold, hard stare. "This book is for babies." Belle slammed the book on the floor and walked into the kitchen.

"Belle!" Garrett called to her. "Get back in here and apologize. What do you say when someone gives you a present?"

"Thanks for the stupid baby book, Charlotte," came the sassy reply from the kitchen. I stood speechless. It was not going at all like I imagined.

Garrett grabbed his jacket and gave the babysitter some last minute instructions. He yelled goodbye to Belle, and we were out the door.

Once we were in the car, Garrett cleared his throat and apologized.

"I'm so sorry about Belle's behaviour. She stayed home from school today because she wasn't feeling well. I think she's just tired and cranky. I almost canceled our plans, but she didn't have a fever or anything. She just needed a break, I think."

"Oh, it's okay, Garrett," I said, unsure that it was. I had no idea what it was like to lose a parent so young. "I imagine it's difficult for her to see her dad with another woman. I'm 32, and I don't know how I would feel if my mom was dating a man that wasn't my father."

"Thank you for being so understanding," Garrett said with thick emotion in his voice. "I owe you one big, sloppy kiss. Maybe two." We laughed.

"I haven't been this happy in a long time, Garrett." I reached across the seat and gave his thigh a reassuring pat. "Everything's gonna be okay," I said with the hope of the ignorant.

But everything was not okay. Half way through our dinner, Garrett got a call from the babysitter. According to the hysterical sitter, Belle threw a tantrum, broke a lamp, and locked herself in her room. Our date was over.

Garrett made excuses for his daughter the whole drive home.

"You know, maybe I should have given her more time before I introduced the two of you. Plus, she's with a new babysitter.

Maybe she just wasn't comfortable. Or maybe it's..." I cut him off.

"What happened to Belle's usual babysitter?" I asked.

"Well, actually, she doesn't have one. I can't seem to get anyone to come back to babysit a second time. Most of them are teenage girls. They just don't know how to handle a nine year old," he concluded.

I thought about those words as we pulled up in front of his house. Maybe it wasn't a nine year old; maybe it was this particular nine year old. A crazy idea came to me.

"Listen, Garrett," I began, "why don't you let me babysit Belle sometime? It would give us a chance to get to know each other without the added pressure of you and a babysitter and the idea of you leaving."

Garrett thought about it for minute.

"Yeah, okay," he said. "I have this all day conference in Baltimore on Saturday. I was hoping this most recent babysitter would watch her, but I don't think that's going to happen after tonight."

"Great!" I said with as much enthusiasm I could muster. "Then I'll see you two Saturday morning!"

Garrett gave me a quick kiss and got out of the car. I watched him jog up to the house and thought, what did I just get myself into?

Saturday morning came with thunder and dark clouds outside my window. I hoped it wasn't an omen. I made some coffee and got myself ready for the day. I wanted to be fully prepared for a visit from a nine year old. I had Harry Potter novels and movies, fresh cookies, and I even downloaded Minecraft onto my iPad, thanks to the suggestion from a trusted friend who taught third grade. I was ready.

Garrett and Belle arrived just as the sky opened and rain poured out from the mouths of the leaden clouds. I opened the door and ushered the wet duo into my foyer.

"Hi, guys!" I said. "Well, this is an eventful beginning to our day, isn't it, Belle?" Belle looked at me and then looked at her dad.

"Do you have to go, Daddy?" she whined.

"Kiddo, we talked about this. I have to go to work. You and Charlotte are going to have lots of fun. I promise!" Garrett knelt in front of Belle and gave her a fierce hug. "Something sure smells good! I think Charlotte made your favourite cookies!" Belle clung tightly to her father. "I'll be back tonight. Now you be a good girl for Charlotte. I love you." Garrett pealed Belle off him as he rose to leave. She crossed her arms and stood in silence. I stood next to her, silently grateful she didn't start screaming.

"Thanks, Charlotte. I hope you two get to know each other a little better today." Garrett gave me a quick peck on the cheek, and he was gone. I closed the door behind him and turned to Belle.

"So, what do you want to do today?" I asked her.

"I don't know. Your house looks boring. Is there any kid stuff here?" Belle looked around and made frowning faces at the obvious lack of a child's presence in my house.

"Well, actually," I began, "I have some Harry Potter movies and books. Have you seen or read any of them?"

I could see a slight interest in her eyes, but she shrugged and said, "Yeah." She released a heavy sigh. "I guess I could watch them again if there's nothing else to do."

"But first, cookies for breakfast!" I said. Belle rolled her eyes at me, but followed me dutifully into the kitchen. She sat at the breakfast bar while I poured her a glass of milk.

She glanced around the kitchen and asked, "Is that a Cookie Monster cookie jar?"

"It is. Cookie Monster was always my favourite Sesame Street character. He was so passionate and didn't seem to care what other people thought," I said with a twinkle, remembering my love of Cookie Monster as a child.

"He's so fat!" Belle exclaimed.

"Well, he eats a lot of cookies," I said.

"Do you eat a lot of cookies?" Belle asked.

"Are you calling me fat?" I half asked, half laughed. Belle shrugged her shoulders. And I thought it was going so well.

"You know who is fat?" I said, quickly changing the subject. "My cat, Stella."

"I don't like cats," Belle said.

"You might like Stella. She's pretty lovable." As if on cue, Stella waddled into the kitchen. I watched Belle watch the cat. Yeah right, she didn't like cats! Belle's eyes grew big and round as she watched Stella saunter over to her food bowl on the floor by the cabinet.

"You weren't kidding! She's huge!" Belle said. "Does she give good hugs? She looks like the kind of cat who would give good hugs."

I swallowed the lump in my throat and said, "Yes, she hugs me more than anyone else in my life."

"Why don't you have any kids, Charlotte? Do you hate kids?" Belle's question took me by surprise. When I didn't answer right away, she added, "Daddy said you don't have any kids and that I shouldn't ask you why not because it's rude and I could make you cry. But I don't care. Because if you don't like kids, then I don't like you." Whoa. This kid had some serious insight for a nine year old. I wondered if losing your mother at such a young age had anything to do with that.

"Well, Sweetie, I do love kids. So much in fact that I was really sad when my husband, Rob, and I didn't have any kids before he passed away." I told her as much of the truth as I could. "But," I continued, "Stella is sort of like our kid. Rob gave her to me on our wedding day."

I decided that was enough sharing for the day. "Let's go watch a movie!" I said as I grabbed the plate of cookies to bring with us into the living room.

The rest of our day was uneventful. Belle and I watched movies (I fell asleep), I read to her (she fell asleep), and I got a lesson on how to tame a cat in Minecraft. Right before Garrett was suppose to pick up Belle, I asked her if she wanted to help me feed Stella.

"Okay!" Bell said. "And you were right, Charlotte. Stella does give really good hugs."

"Oh, yeah?" I smiled. "How do you know that?"

"Well, when you were sleeping, I got kinda bored, so I went in your room and gave Stella some hugs."

"I bet she loved that, Belle. Now let's go find her so she can eat!" Our day together turned out so much better than I could have imagined. She even took my hand as we went in search of Stella. Belle and I walked into the bedroom together, but what I saw on my bed made me immediately drop the little girl's hand.

Stella's body was twisted into an awkward contortion of limbs and fur. Her eyes bulged out of her head at three times their normal size.

"What did you do, Belle?" I whispered.

"I don't know! I just gave her a couple squeezes!" she said. I knelt down in front of Belle and grabbed her arms.

"You... little... monster!" I yelled in her face. "You killed my baby! You killed..." I couldn't even get the words out. I collapsed to the floor. Belle just stood there, staring at Stella's dead body.

This was how Garrett found us. I heard his voice, but the words were a muffled noise in my brain. He spoke to Belle. He tried to speak to me. Finally, I heard him saying my name.

"Charlotte!" he said. "Charlotte! Look at me! What happened?"

I raised my head to make eye contact. "Get that child out of my house," was all I said. Garrett looked shocked, but he didn't move. "Get out! Get out! Get out!" I screeched.

Garrett and Belle left me alone. I stayed on the floor all night. I cried over every memory I could muster about Stella, about Rob, and about the things I could never get back.

When morning came, I thought about Garrett and how much I loved him. I thought about Belle and the way I treated her. I was angry, hurt, and humiliated. She was just a kid who lost her mother, and I had said terrible things to her.

I couldn't pick up the phone to call Garrett, but I did go to our next therapy session. I wasn't sure what he would say to me, but I needed the comfort of the group. I had grown to depend on them more than I realized.

When I arrived at the church, Garrett was waiting for me in the main foyer.

"Charlotte," he cleared his throat and said, "Look, I wanted to call you, but I wasn't sure if you would even talk to me." His face was unshaven. His hair was disheveled. He ran his hand through his hair, and I noticed he wasn't wearing his wedding ring. My mind flashed back to that first day we met. I had no idea how important this man in front of me would become. I looked down at my naked ring finger and smiled.

Garrett took my smile as a sign to continue his speech.

"I know what happened to Stella is awful. And I could never replace her or what she meant to you." His voice broke as he tried to clear his throat, but it didn't matter; I was already crying. "But what I want to tell you is this—after we left your house Saturday night, Belle told me about your day together. She was pretty upset, of course, but she told me she hadn't been that happy since her mother was alive." Garrett finished his last sentence as tears ran down his face. We didn't care that we looked ridiculous, standing there in the middle of a church, crying over what we lost and what we could still gain from each other. I put my hands on his face.

"I love you." I paused. "So much," I told him. Garrett pulled away and fished something out of his pocket. When he got down on one knee, I looked around and realized everyone from our therapy group watched from the hallway.

"Charlotte, I know we haven't known each other long enough, but we've known each other strong enough. And that's more than enough for me. Will you marry me? Will you be my wife and a mother to Belle?"

"Yes," I said. "I would be honoured to be a part of your family."

Garrett gave me a deep, intimate kiss right there in the middle of the church. Everyone from therapy started clapping and came over to congratulate us. Alice hugged me tightly. Joe shook Garrett's hand. And just like that first night, I had to excuse myself to the bathroom to wipe my tears.

Our engagement was short. We didn't want a big, fancy wedding. We wanted something small, intimate and perfect. We did, of course, invite everyone from therapy, but they were half the guest list.

We got married at the diner where we had our first cup of coffee. The owner let us rent the large room in the back and even gave us a discount on the food. We didn't need white dresses or tuxedos, bridesmaids or groomsmen—just Garrett, Belle, and me standing before Joe, who got ordained online so he could marry us. My friend who taught third grade offered to take pictures.

After we exchanged our vows, we positioned ourselves for a family picture. Belle tugged my sleeve and motioned for me to bend down. She whispered in my ear so only I could hear her.

"I just want you to know I killed Stella on purpose. I hate you, Charlotte. You will never be my mommy." Just as the true horror of Belle's words hit me, the camera flashed in our eyes.

"But why, Belle?" I said.

"Because," she smirked, "Like you said... I'm a monster."

SOCIAL MURDERER
BY CARL BAUMANN

Why is my phone wearing a shoe?
I was struggling to look at the screen through a red haze. *I must have drunk WAY too much last night.* I'd been at Mitch's stag party and hoping I was sober enough to escape a DUI. I tried to blink away the sticky sleep from my eyes. I peered closer at the phone in my hand that seemed to be constantly ringing and buzzing.

That can't be right? My cell phone appeared to have metamorphosed into a shoe. My shoe. And it had my sock in it. The green socks with yellow diamonds I'd been wearing last night. And the sock wasn't empty. It had a foot in it. My foot! Raggedly severed with bone protruding from the stump. I screamed and dropped the revolting object. It fell up and thudded loudly on the ceiling. *Fell up?* I suddenly realized I wasn't in bed but suspended upside down in my car. Screaming at the top of my lungs for help, I failed to see the hand reaching in to retrieve my foot.

I had been a late-comer to social media. Working as a Senior Counsellor at a mental health service in Richmond, Virginia for

175

the past fifteen years left me too drained for internet nonsense. Fifteen years is a damn long time to be surrounded by the mentally ill. The patients weren't much better, I laughed to myself. I had a busy work and home life and had always considered the all-pervasive apps a complete waste of time. Too many people just living through the screens of their mobile devices instead of actually doing things and interacting with real people. But Michela, my teenage brat daughter, took the piss and insisted on calling me old-fashioned and boring. This, coupled with the fact that my patients seemed obsessed with these apps and constantly referred to them in our sessions, finally compelled me to open accounts and explore the digital world. I found it ironic, and more than a little irritating, that Michela failed to acknowledge my friend request. *Little bitch.*

All too quickly, I found myself drawn in. Old colleagues, school and college friends plus distant family members inundated me with friend requests and all kinds of pointless crap. Constant comments on their lives, political opinions, pictures of what they ate for dinner or which airport they were currently at. With my background in psychology I found these insights into human behaviour, no matter how trivial or annoying, fascinating. So I threw myself in at the deep end. Studied people's behaviour on the web. Read about trolls and Internet stalkers. Learned how easily people could be manipulated by strangers to commit suicide or murder. These modern day monsters were just random voices in the electronic wilderness, hell-bent on causing misery just because they could. These creeps considered themselves anonymous and untouchable. They had no fear of being discovered or having a victim appear on their door-step carrying a hatchet. This dark side of the net intrigued and tempted me. I started wondering how easy it would be to join their ranks. *Could I be that evil? And how much fun could it be?*

Although I am an expert in treating obsessive, compulsive behaviour and traits, I failed to recognize these starting to impinge on my own life. Eventually I couldn't bear to be parted from my cell phone, tablet or laptop and I even interrupted my sessions with patients to check for new updates and messages. My downfall would be to finally create my own support group, specifically for people suffering from bipolar disorder.

I was compelled to be there twenty-four seven. I was the Admin and needed to moderate and help those in crisis. Everything else became irrelevant. I had to be available. It was my child and I needed to nurture it. The compassion that had drawn me to the healing profession now spread across the globe. I couldn't refuse any request for assistance or advice from anyone, anywhere, anytime. I wouldn't even drive without my phone glued to the windshield. Just in case I missed a cry for help. That was why I failed to see the trap on the bridge. The spring-loaded device that spun my car over the edge and left it crumpled on its roof next to the river. Ripping the foot off my leg in the process.

But eventually these constant demands for assistance started to bore me. They became repetitive and began to frustrate. My advice was ignored. And I *hate* being ignored. The same damn people coming back to me every day with the same damn problems. And they were always trivial and mundane. Easily resolvable if they could be bothered to help themselves rather than bleat on looking for sympathy. That was how I started to feel anyway. *There can be a fine line between being in need of help and just being boring.*

So I decided to liven things up. I knew the buttons to press. My advice stayed the same. Almost. Disguised among the sympathetic words I began to sow seeds of dissension. Subliminal messages and wordings that I knew would eat like maggots within the already twisted minds of my readers. *The ultimate social experiment - winky face.* Just suggestions that maybe their lives would improve without the influence of their friends and family. Perhaps simple solutions could be found for the removal of their problems? I would suggest that they should move on. And moving is much easier when you have no baggage to take with you. You can erase the past. Perhaps *rub* it out?

Keeping track of my success was easy. My group member's status updates became more interesting. Especially when they were dead or incarcerated. Their family members kept the accounts open and posted condolences or information about their absence from social media. Often I could find out where my members were being held and send traditional snail mail to them in order to continue giving *help*. Then it was just a case of watching the news and reading the obituary columns.

I was unable to believe my luck when I came across Ryan Punches. The young man came from a troubled, redneck, family and lived in a backwater of Okeechobee. When Ryan private messaged me I could almost hear the duelling banjos from Deliverance trilling in my ears. Manipulating Ryan was easier than the apple pie he undoubtedly ate every day. First I requested that Ryan keep a daily diary of his mood swings and triggers. He was to email them to me as often as possible. I gave my advice for free. A service that the young man would never have been able to obtain within the good old U.S. of A.'s medical system.

Over the course of a few weeks our relationship developed. A bond formed between us. Ryan had never received such concerned, fatherly, advice. He told me that the only pearls of wisdom he'd received from his mother's frequently changing boyfriends had been delivered by the end of a belt. Not a comforting, re-assuring, email each night. He was more than willing to take my every advisement at face value, and told me that he often wept into his pillow at night for the kindness he was receiving. That made me laugh. If the only the slow-witted fool had known he was just a pawn in my game.

I slowly managed to convince Ryan that his problems were not of his own making. His mother and five older brothers were the ones to blame. They should be the ones to pay. They deserved it. They needed to be taught the error of their ways. It was only right. God would forgive him, I said. He could be a tool of righteous justice. Just like overturning the money-lenders tables in the temple, Ryan could be the lesson that the unworthy and mean members of his family needed to learn.

But how? Ryan asked me. They're big and tough. These guys bite the heads off rattlesnakes just for fun and to impress the waitresses at the local bar. They know I'm a pussy, he said. A wimp. They wipe their boots on me when they get back from the mill. What can *I* do?

You have brains, I told him. You have a soul. It will be easy. And it was easy – thank you Internet! I spent a fruitful five minutes researching bomb-making. Then I instructed him on what to buy at his local Kmart. What amount of gas to get at the gas station and in what type of containers to store it. I walked him through constructing the bombs and where best to place them in the crawl space beneath his family's trailer home. All that Ryan need do was set the device's timers and go to church to pray. I assured Ryan that when he left for the evening service his redemption would be secured. Easy.

I treated myself to a huge surf 'n' turf and a pitcher of Margaritas the night that Ryan had told me he was going to church the next day. Even though I'd been saving myself for Mitch's stag party the next night. The news would make national broadcasts. CNN, NBC. Maybe even the BBC! I toasted myself. *That poor sap Ryan – sad face.* After checking his computer, the FBI would undoubtedly come to me for my professional assessment of his mental state. The key words were already flowing through my mind. Delusional. Paranoid. Religious fixations. Extremely unstable. Anger management issues. Abused. The list went on and on. "I tried my best!" I would decry. "But there was only so much I could do over the Internet." *If only they knew...*

I had chuckled to myself. *Maybe it's the booze?* It wasn't though. It was the thought that my next group member's actions would eclipse Ryan Punches' with a dark shadow that may never be lifted. I'd already started grooming a disturbed young woman in Boston, Massachusetts. *Smiley face...*

I was shocked awake and screamed at the top of my lungs when Ryan banged a hot skillet against the end of my right leg. The one that was missing a foot. The foot that had been torn off by the accelerator pedal when Ryan's trap blew my car off the road. Panicking, I looked left and right. All I could see through the pain were semi-circles of light far off to each side. Just dark, damp, brick-work above. The stench of a sewage adulterated brook assaulted my nostrils. I puked all down the front of my shirt. I tried desperately to wipe my face but my hands were tied behind my back. "Where the hell am I?" I choked.

"You're in my home." Ryan answered. His voice was deep and gravelly. *Very* deep. Yet also strangely feminine.

"Who are you?" I cried, delirious. "What happened? Why aren't I in the hospital?"

"I thought it was about time we met face-to-face. I'm Ryan Punches. Well, that's who you think I am."

"Ryan? Ryan from the group? *My* Ryan?" I forgot my agony for a second. This was insane. Ryan lived hundreds of miles away. He should be in jail by now. Or an asylum. This wasn't possible. And what was that delicious smell of something cooking?

"I'm not *your* Ryan, Andy. I'm your troll."

I started to doubt my own sanity. "You're my troll? What are you talking about? You mean on the Internet? You've been trolling me?" This didn't make sense. If anything, I'd been trolling Ryan.

The young man sighed. "No Andy. I'm a troll who uses the Internet. Look around. This is where I live. You drive over me every day on the way home."

I took a moment to examine my surroundings more closely. We were under a bridge. And there was a pot bubbling over a fire between us. That's where the smell making me salivate was coming from. I stared at Ryan. Just a youth with sandy hair, wearing a checked shirt and jeans, holding a smart-phone. The same person whose profile picture was on his personal page. Then Ryan shimmered. I blinked. Now there was a dumpy middle-aged woman sitting opposite me. Wearing a tartan skirt and with a laptop perched on her ample lap. She winked at me. *What the hell?* A second shimmer. I voided my bowels. The thing's head almost touched the ceiling. It was covered in fur the colour of moss. And it had tusks. *Oh my God. It's mouth! And is that my fucking laptop it's holding?* I gagged from the stench of shit emanating from the brook and my pants. "You're telling me you're a troll. A *real* troll? The kind of troll that snatches people and eats them?"

"Almost right Andy. But we're a bit savvier in this Internet age. Rather than wait for unsuspecting travellers, we find you online now. So we know you're *deserving*. And we don't eat you. We make you eat yourselves. Personally I prefer fried chicken." The troll stuck a fork in the pot and pulled out my foot. He waved it underneath my nose. "Don't worry though. You're not going to die today."

I stared in horror at the meat that was slowly falling away from the bones. Despite myself I licked my lips. "No? So you're going to let me go if I eat *that?*"

"Don't be silly Andy. I said you weren't going to die *today*. This will take months." It winked again. "Look on the bright side though. You won't go hungry."

About the Authors

And now, about the Authors, in their own words. Please make sure to check out the ones you like and the ones that made you think.

◆ CHRIS MUSGRAVE

Chris Musgrave has always enjoyed a good story, so much so that he's spent the last twenty years trying to write one of his own. His passion is for horror but he's just as content with a good urban fantasy or speculative fiction.

He lives in Yorkshire — a remote area in the north of the United Kingdom known for its tea and strange wildlife — with his wife, his son, and an army of freeloaders which he kindly refers to as 'characters'.

When he's not writing fiction, he's blogging over at www.chrismusgravewriter.com or as a contributor at www.thesarcasticmuse.com.

◆ JOHN RYERS

John hails from Ontario, Canada with his wife and twin daughters. He's written fantasy from a very young age, inspired by the impromptu stories told by his father at bedtime. In 2012, John created the realm of Aeryeth, a fantasy world set in medieval times and ruled by elemental magic. His debut novel The Glass Thief is slated for release in late 2016.

Find out more about John at: johnryers.com

◆ DAVID WILEY

David Wiley is an author of science fiction and fantasy stories, choosing to write the stories that he would love to read.

His short fiction has previously been published in Sci Phi Journal, OWS Ink, Mystic Signals and King Arthur anthologies by Uffda Press and 18th Wall Productions. David resides in central Iowa with his wife and their cats and spends his time reading, writing, and playing board games.

◆ P.A. CORNELL

P.A. Cornell is a reformed journalist and copy editor who now dedicates her writing life to fiction. As a graduate of the Odyssey Writing Workshop (Class of 2002) she prefers writing genre fiction which allows her imagination to run wild. This is the first story she has written in the horror genre. She lives in Hamilton, Ontario, with her husband and their three little "monsters."

◆ TONY J. LYNCH-BRADISH

Toni J Lynch-Bradish is a Contemporary Fiction writer and blogger with a love for short stories living in Northwest Ohio with her three children and loving hubby. She has been a writer since she can remember and although she put it aside for many years she has realized that it is her calling in life to bring characters and their stories into existence. Also an avid reader and lover of miniatures; when she isn't writing she is usually seen with a book in one hand and a glue gun in the other.

◆ C.P. ROELKE

C.P. Roelke predominately writes fantasy horror set in modern times, but he also enjoys branching out into other genres. When not writing, he spends his free time exploring the Alaskan outdoors and playing board games with family and friends. You can follow him on Twitter by going to twitter.com/cproelke.

◆ STEPHANIE AYERS

A published author with a knack for twisted tales, Stephanie Ayers is the CEO of Our Write Side, a community for writers and readers alike. She loves a good thriller, things that go bump in the night, and sappy stories.

◆ R.G. WESTERMAN

Ms. Westerman lives in the mountains of East Tennessee with her gorgeous husband and her two genius children. Her background is in Theatre and she has an M.A. in Marketing, but her passion is the written word. She loves to write about the strange and unusual, and her latest serial, The Rising Ash Saga, can be found on Amazon. She can also be found in various corners of the internet on Facebook at R.G. Westerman. Follow her on Twitter, @rgwesterman, and at her Amazon author page under R.G. Westerman.

◆ LAURA JOHNSON

Laura Johnson is a fantasy writer and poet who hails from Toronto, Canada. Although her Psychology degree doesn't give her the ability to read minds, she does use it to flesh out her characters. Her writing lair is littered with dragon paraphernalia, emergency rations of dark chocolate, and enough books to fill a small library. At present she is working on a fantasy series that blends intrigue, mythology, and dark magic. Previously, her work has appeared two anthologies: Folklore, a collection of poems and short stories about Scandinavian folklore, and Heroes, a book of superhero-themed tales.

◆ SARAH ROBERTSON

Sarah Robertson, wife of Brian Robertson, specializes in post-apocalyptic skills including, but not limited to: knitting, crocheting, running, swing dancing, making delicious coffee, and living in Colorado. She also considers herself quite proficient in smiling, making new friends, and conquering the world.

◆ TYLER OMICHINSKI

Tyler is a writer, editor, and game designer from the wild wastes of Canada. His work has been published in the Ennie Award Nominated Protodimension, his Ultimate Celts Guide has been a bestseller, and more. He also serves as the Executive Editor and Co-Host at Comix I Read.

His work and portfolio, as well as random musings, can be found at www.omichinski.com

◆ PAUL R. DAVIS

With the experiences of mission trips to Guatemala, international travel, a Tough Mudder, teaching in Kentucky and Wisconsin, and a few forced experiences out in mother nature, Paul R Davis seeks to put the excitement of life in his books, inspiring others to seek adventure.

storytellerdavis.wordpress.com

◆ S.F. GEBEL

I believe the worst monsters are the ones we create ourselves, and the most damaging tragedies are the ones we inflict on ourselves. Everything in this story was said by me, to me, or about me... with some creative exaggeration. I currently teach high school English and college composition, while writing. I write fantasy, dystopian, and other forms of fiction. This story marks my first publication, and I look forward to many more to come. Check out my blog where I write reviews and posts about my writing and life: www.readingwithhighlighters.wordpress.com

◆ N.E. HARVEY

N.E. Harvey is an author, poet, and writer of all things dark and chilling – focusing on horror, paranormal thriller and dark fantasy genres.
She lives in Buckinghamshire, England with her fiancé and their rapidly growing book collection. When she is not making up twisted poems and stories that make people fear for her sanity, she is studying for a degree, blogging, reading as many books as she can get her hands on or, for the most part, procrastinating at Grandmaster level.
You can find her online at www.traineeauthor.wordpress.com.

◆ BECCA ODELIUS

On most days, Becca Odelius can be found living a full life inside her own head. She loves creating stories with strange characters and unique twists. Her passions include crossword puzzles, hiding from strangers, and one day moving to the west coast. She is an avid reader of books made of paper and holds a BA in English Literature from Goucher College. She currently resides in a Baltimore suburb with her husband, four daughters, two cats, and one very ornery step-dog.

◆ CARL BAUMANN

Saint or Sinner? – Depends on who you ask. Fluffy, innocent and benevolent are sometimes used when describing Carl and his work. But only by people who have been looking in completely the wrong direction. Mentally unwell, manipulative, loving father, fetish club performer and promoter, swimming teacher, IT professional – all true... And then there's the rest. Step into his club, just keep a hold of your wallet or purse.

www.spykeyone.com

About the Editor

◆ ASHLEY CYR

It didn't take long after graduating from the Queen's University for Ashley Cyr to jump into publishing with both feet. By day she works at an academic publishing house, while by night she is the Editor in Chief at Bushmead Publishing. She has served as editor for best-selling novels, and has served as primary editor for Heroes, Monsters, and Another Place.

You can follow the work that she does at Bushmead by going to www.bushmead.com

www.ingramcontent.com/pod-product-compliance
Lightning Source LLC
Chambersburg PA
CBHW060222180626
46813CB00007B/2923